I0577604

ALEX CAGE
CLEAN FAST-PACED ACTION THRILLERS

JOIN THE READER'S LIST

Get the latest releases and exclusive giveaways - sign up to the Alex Cage Reader List:

www.AlexCage.com/signup

ALSO BY ALEX CAGE

Orlando Black Series

Carolina Dance

Bayside Boom

Family Famous (Novella)

Bet on Black

Leroy Silver Series

Contracts & Bullets

Aloha & Bullets

Politics Thieves & Bullets

READING ORDER

The heart-stopping, action-packed Orlando Black books can be read in any order, but are best enjoyed in the following sequence:

Carolina Dance (Book1)

Queen City Ruby (Short Story)

Survival Intuition (A Rose Lee Flash Fiction Story) *

Sunshine Scandal (Short Story)

Once You Go Black (Short Story)

Bayside Boom (Book 2)

Family Famous (Novella)

Bet on Black (Book 3)

* Currently the eBook, Survival Intuition, is only available to A+ members on the Alex Cage Reader's list.

You can sign up for a free read and an opportunity for A+ status: www.AlexCage.com/signup

FAMILY FAMOUS

AN ORLANDO BLACK STORY

ALEX CAGE

FAMILY FAMOUS

FAMILY FAMOUS

THERE WERE THREE kidnappers, a woman, and two men. They sat inside a parked Crown Victoria, looking out into the early morning darkness at a bar across Sunset Boulevard. The woman sat behind the wheel, and the men lounged on the passenger side, one in the front and the other in the back. The car's floorboard was littered with wrappers and fumed with the smell of takeout.

The man in the back seat crossed his arms and sighed. "Are you sure he's here?" he asked the woman.

She whipped her silky black hair over her shoulder and looked at him with penetrating brown eyes. "No, Phil. I just happen to like this bar."

"I'm only asking because we've been here for hours. No need to get rude."

The man in the front threw his bulky arm over the seat and twisted his body to look at Phil. He shook his head before turning back. "Amateur," he said in a slight Spanish accent.

"Amateur?" Phil replied. "I'm the only one here with formal law enforcement training," he boasted.

"That makes you the least qualified for this."

"What was that, Lucas?"

"You heard me, *güero*."

"What did you call me?"

"Boys, boys," the woman said. "There he goes," she continued, pointing across Lucas and out the window.

From the bar staggered a slender, dark-skinned man. He wore a dingy, yellow shirt halfway tucked inside, a pair of blue slacks torn at the thigh. The soles of his brown dress shoes flapped with each step.

"This is the guy that's worth millions?" Phil asked with a slight chuckle.

Lucas took in a breath and exhaled sharply while looking at the woman.

She raised her palm, gesturing for him to keep his cool. At that, Lucas looked out his window toward the drunken man, and the woman at the wheel turned to Phil with a smirk cutting into her cheek.

"Why don't you let mom and dad handle this? You just sit back there and be a good boy. Okay, Phillip?"

Phil tilted his head. "Interesting," he said, squinting. "Mom and dad asked for my help. Plus, I'm not the one who has fallen from the cartel's grace. Am I, Eva?"

She stared at him hard. Winkles began to expel the smooth skin from her light-brown face, and her nose crinkled, exposing some of her tiny, white teeth.

Phil stared back but noticed Eva's hand creeping close to her waist. Her motion ceased as Lucas interrupted.

"It's clear. If we're going to do this, we better do it now," he said.

Eva fixed on Phil for another second before turning to face the wheel. She fired up the car and threw it into gear before performing a maneuver that ended with the Crown Vic on the opposite side of the street, stopped in front of the inebriated man.

Lucas and Phil sprung from the car and dashed to the

wobbling man. Lucas grabbed him from the left and Phil from the right.

"Oh, this guy smells like a beer factory," Phil commented, wincing as they pushed the guy toward the car.

"Just get him inside," Lucas said.

The man stumbled along. "Hey—wh-wha-wh-where you take me?" was all he asked in a slurred British accent as they shoved him into the back of the Crown Victoria.

"He's in. Let's go, let's go!" Phil said, closing the back passenger side door.

Eva floored the gas pedal, sending the Crown Vic racing down the road.

SIX HOURS LATER, Orlando Black was driving on that same street. He enjoyed the sight of the palm trees rolling by with the Hollywood sign at the top of the mountain in the distance. What he wasn't enjoying was stopping every thirty seconds for a traffic light and the horns and revving engines of morning traffic.

This is what I get for taking the scenic route, he thought.

His plan was to continue south to San Diego, then head east through Arizona. He had a full tank of gas, but his stomach was running on empty. Black remembered days in the military when meals were infrequent, so better eat while you have the chance became his philosophy. The same with rest and sleep.

After another mile of driving, he whipped the Viper GTS into the parking lot of a popular cafe. The restaurant was a small building that sat directly off the main road. He closed his car door and crunched across the gravel parking lot toward the entrance, where a man in a loosely fitted suit with slick dark hair addressed him.

"A Viper. You don't see many of those anymore," the man said, holding his chin. "It's black too. Hot car."

Black hunched his shoulders. "Thanks."

The guy crossed his arms. "I have one of the new E-Class Mercedes Benz," he said, tilting his head in the car's direction.

Black looked in that direction and saw a brand new, silver coupe. "Nice car," he said.

The slick-haired man smirked. "It cost sixty thousand dollars—it better be."

Black gave him a quick nod and turned toward the restaurant.

"I have great credit, so the bank didn't mind loaning me the money," the man continued.

Black sighed and looked over his shoulder.

The guy in the suit was nodding, arms still folded and a grin on his face.

Black shrugged, softly shaking his head before continuing to the restaurant and leaving the man standing in the parking lot. *The superficial capital of the world,* he thought.

He stepped off the gravel and onto the sidewalk leading to the front door where a large sign that read Ralph's Donut House hung above. The inside of the cafe greeted him with aromas of coffee and pastries and the clinking of cookware. The dining area had little seating, and there weren't many customers, so it was easy for Black to order a breakfast sandwich, water, and black coffee before sliding into a booth facing the front entrance and an overhead TV.

The news was on, and a clean shaved reporter with salt-and-pepper hair talked about the politics in Washington.

"The White House reported the president's staff is rethinking Public Law 324," the news anchor said. "It appears to be causing more unrest than his advisors expected."

Black chuckled to himself. "No kidding," he muttered, turning his attention to his breakfast.

He cleared his plate just in time to catch the tail end of the weather segment. The meteorologist forecasted comfortable day temperatures and cool night temperatures for the rest of the week. He then turned the broadcast over to his colleague to cover celebrity news, and a fair-skinned woman with a head full of blonde hair appeared on the screen.

"We'll begin with the story everyone is talking about," she said. "The lady who has been a major headline over the past couple of weeks, Chasity Fox."

The TV flicked to a video of a skimpily dressed young woman dancing on stage. The camera zoomed in closer, revealing her dark olive skin and toned physique as she brushed her highlighted hair behind her ear. The screen then displayed a closeup of the performer's face next to an older woman's face, and the reporter started talking again.

"Many are wondering what happened between the pop artist and her mother slash ex-manager. In an interview, Fox stated she fired her mother because of irreconcilable differences, but some believe the split was financially motivated. It makes sense considering she's worth over a hundred million…"

Black ignored the TV for a few moments as he finished drinking his water. Once done, he glanced at the screen again to find a shot of the young lady hugging an athletic guy with electric blue eyes and brushed up dirty blond hair. The headline underneath read, *Boyfriend Problems*. Black shook his head and focused on his cup of coffee before taking a sip. Ten minutes passed before his cup was empty, and as he considered getting a cup to go, two people entered the cafe. The first was an apple body shaped woman, with short brown hair and matching brown eyes behind her glasses. Coming in after her was another woman wearing dark shades and a purple hoodie, the hood covering her head. The two made their way down the narrow aisle and found a booth diagonally across from Black.

"Is this okay here?" the woman with glasses asked the one with the hoodie.

The lady in the hoodie nodded slightly and moved her lips, but nothing came out.

"Chas, is this okay?" the one with glasses asked again, louder.

The one called Chas craned toward her friend and looked her in the eyes. "Yesss, Bridget," she said with a British accent and a smile on her face.

"Whatever."

The two women laughed as they settled into the booth. Bridget faced Black, and the other woman had her back to him. Chas removed her shades, and the hood from her head then began conversing with her friend.

Black shrugged and looked at the TV, still deciding if he wanted to take a cup of coffee to go.

A minute later, Bridget stood and walked past him toward the restrooms. As she did, her friend turned and looked in that direction.

Black locked eyes with her and was surprised when he recognized who she was. *Miss Major Headline, Chasity Fox.* She had straight black hair highlighted with various shades of blue, the same as on TV. She looked fit, but her cheeks were a little puffy, and circles like faded bruises underscored her eyes.

She jolted her head and turned to face her table.

Black looked at his empty coffee cup and decided he'd had enough. He eased out of the booth before leaving a tip on his table and started toward the front door. As he stepped past Chasity's booth, she slid out, running into his shoulder.

She staggered backward, but Black caught her. "You okay?" he asked, holding her in his arms.

"Yeah, I'm so sorry," she said, looking up at him. "I'm a bit out of it. Lot's going on," she finished with a nervous smile.

Black released her, and they stared at each other for a moment. He pressed his lips together and briefly glanced at the front door. She looked away momentarily before fixing on his face once again.

"I—um," Black struggled for words. "You know… things have a way of working out," he finally said.

Chasity lifted her eyebrows and simpered, staring at him.

"Have a good day," Black said, brushing past her.

He felt her eyes on his back as he walked to the door. When he stepped outside, he noticed a dark blue Crown Vic with tinted windows parked at the curb a few paces from the front of the restaurant. He continued up the empty sidewalk, just past the parked Crown Vic, before hearing the door to the restaurant open behind him.

"Hey, excuse me," a voice called.

Black turned to find Chasity walking to him.

"Hi, I'm sorry, who are you?" she asked.

He squinted at the question. "Excuse me?"

"I know it's weird, but I just want to know your name."

The two locked eyes again, and Black was about to share his name but noticed the Crown Vic's front and back passenger doors swing open. Two figures rushed toward him and Chasity. The first was a thin, pale man coming up behind Chasity, and the second was a burly Hispanic male advancing from Black's right.

Chasity gasped as the thin man placed his hand on her shoulder.

Black took a step forward but stopped when he saw what was in the man's hand. From his hip, he held a silver pistol aimed at Chasity's lower back.

The stocky guy stuck the muzzle of his gun in Black's side. "Everybody be cool, and no one gets hurt," he instructed.

"That's right," the pale guy said. "We're going for a ride," he continued, pulling Chasity toward the back car door.

He slid into the back seat with his gun still trained on Chasity. Once inside the car, he waved her in with the gun.

"You too," the Latino man said, shoving Black toward the back door.

Black turned and glared at the man.

He raised his gun to Black's chest. "Get in before we have a problem."

Black looked down at the gun, then at the man's face again. *You already got a problem,* he thought, cocking an eyebrow before ducking into the backseat as the door shut beside him.

The smell of french fries and Chinese food filled the car's dim interior.

Chasity sat in the middle seat, doing her best to lean closer toward Black avoiding any physical contact with her kidnapper on the opposite side.

The burly guy jumped in the front passenger seat, and the car spun off, swerving into traffic as car horns blew from behind.

Chasity's breathing became louder with each exhale. Black touched her hand to calm her. He looked to the front and saw a petite, Hispanic woman at the wheel and the barrel of a gun aimed at him by the front passenger.

"Just sit back and be quiet," the bulky man said.

THEY DROVE A few blocks before parking in an abandoned shopping center. The woman at the wheel removed the key from the ignition and turned, giving Black a glance before fixing on Chasity.

"Hi, Señorita Fox," she said.

"Do I know you? Who are you?" Chasity asked with wrinkled eyebrows and a slight head shake.

"Just a businesswoman. Who's this?" the lady up front asked, tilting her head at Black.

"He's just my… my bodyguard."

"Not a very good one," the Hispanic man said, gun still trained on Black.

Black looked at him but said nothing.

"What do you want with me?" Chasity asked the lady at the wheel.

"I have a business proposition for you," the woman said, grinning.

"I don't understand."

"Let me help you, *mami*," she said, handing Chasity a phone.

Chasity looked at the screen. Her eyes widened, and her mouth gaped open. Black couldn't make out what was on the screen from his vantage point.

The woman snatched the phone from Chasity. "You have thirty-six hours to get me twenty million in cash," she said.

"I—I can't. How can I?" Chasity protested.

"If you don't, someone might have an accident."

Chasity sat with her mouth open.

"Nod if you understand."

Chasity slowly nodded.

"Good. We'll be in contact," the woman said, handing Chasity a flip phone. "Oh, and if I suspect you've called the cops—well, like I said, accidents happen," she concluded, turning to face the steering wheel.

"Now, both of you out," the burly guy said.

Black reached for the door handle.

"See you around, bodyguard," the man up front mocked.

I look forward to it, Black thought, glaring at him before opening the door and stepping onto the pavement.

He helped Chasity out of the car, catching her in his arms as the door slammed shut and the car circled the parking lot.

"Friends of yours?" he asked her, watching as the car sped out of the shopping center.

When she didn't answer, he looked at her. She had her

face buried down near his chest. He nudged her to an arm's length.

"Chasity, who were those people?"

She shook her head, "I don't know," she sobbed, looking up at him with tears.

He said nothing, just stared at her.

She hunched her shoulders. "Seriously, I really don't know," she said, inspecting the flip phone in her hand before stuffing it in her pocket.

"Well, they sure know you," Black said, pivoting in the direction the car left.

He turned to Chasity to see she was examining her smartphone.

"Great... Bridget called me three times. She probably thinks I ditched her," she said.

"Okay, I guess we better get you back then," Black said, nodding in the sidewalk's direction.

On the walk back, Chasity tried calling Bridget but didn't get her.

"I hope she's okay," she told Black. "You don't think they have her, do you?"

"Don't worry, she's fine," he answered over the bustle of passing traffic.

"How can you be so sure? I can't believe this is happening. I'm so sorry I got you mixed up in this—"

Black touched her shoulder, and the two stopped walking as he did.

"Take a deep breath," he said.

Chasity closed her eyes, inhaled slowly, and rushed an exhale before opening them again.

"Getting yourself worked up won't help."

Chasity nodded. "I know," she said in a soft tone.

"They showed you a picture of something. What was it?" Black asked.

She looked at the ground, bit her top lip, and continued up the sidewalk without answering.

Black shrugged. "Okay then," he said, pacing a few steps behind her.

The ten-minute walk back to the cafe was quiet. Chasity kept her head down for most of it, stuck in her thoughts, Black figured.

She looked at the restaurant's parking lot. "Great, I don't see Bridget's car. Let me try her again," she said, removing her cell phone and poking at it.

Black left her on the sidewalk and entered the cafe. He purchased two bottles of water before returning to find her pocketing her phone and releasing a deep sigh.

He walked over. "I take it you didn't get her," he said, handing her a bottle of water.

She shook her head, "No," she muttered, taking the water and staring down at the pavement.

Black took a swig of his water.

"I have a favor to ask," she said, looking up.

He removed the bottle from his lips but said nothing, just waited for her to ask.

"Could you take me to Beverly Hills?"

"Sure, but what's in Beverly Hills?"

"My—my mother."

"I see. I'm over here," he said, pointing his thumb in the direction of the parking lot.

When they entered the car, Black started the engine and noticed Chasity gazing at him.

"What?" he asked.

"I just realized something," she said. "You know who I am, but I don't know your name."

"My name is *bodyguard*, remember?" Black said.

Chasity chuckled. "I'm sorry, that's all I could think to tell them," she said. "But really, what's your name? I want to know."

"Orlando Black," he answered, putting the car in gear and driving toward the parking lot's exit.

Chasity instructed him to make a left, and they drove for a few minutes before she directed him into a right turn.

"We'll be on this road for a while," she said. "So—Mr. Black, tell me about yourself."

"What do you want to know?"

"Let's see. How about… where are you from?"

"All over."

"Well, where do you currently live?"

"Nowhere."

"What?"

"I sold my home a little while back."

"Okay—are you from around here?"

"You can say that. I spent a lot of my teenage years in California."

"So, you grew up around here, purchased a home, then sold it, and now what?"

"Not exactly."

"Oh boy. Getting information from you is like pulling teeth, Black."

Black glanced at her before placing his sights back on the road. "Sorry. It's sort of a habit," he said. "To make a long story short, I graduated from school while here in California. Then I went into the military. After the military, I moved around Asia for some time before coming back to the States."

Chasity rested the side of her cheek in her hand and stared at him. "Wow, Asia. Life is different in those countries. I really love it in Japan," she said with a smile. "So, you came back to the States and purchased a home here in California?"

"Nope, North Carolina."

"What made you want to leave there?" she asked, squinting.

"A change of scenery."

"I mean—who—where do you work? How do you make a living?"

"I manage, but enough about me. Are you going to share what's going on?"

Chasity adjusted in her seat. "I knew you would bring that up."

"When I'm held at gunpoint, I want to know why."

"They want me to pay them twenty million in cash."

"I know that much. My question is why. What was in that picture?"

Chasity exhaled. "They have… they have my father."

Black looked at her. She was facing the windshield, gazing out at the road, teary-eyed.

"You two are close?" he asked.

She nodded. "We were very close, but I don't want to talk about it right now."

Black shrugged without looking at Chasity. "I understand," he said.

THE NEXT TEN minutes of the drive were quiet. Black and Chasity looked straight ahead, watching as Mercedes-Benzes and Porsches entered and exited the street and the buildings and palm trees passed by. Slowly, traffic thinned, and the buildings disappeared as the tall fan palms continued to roll by.

Chasity retrieved her cell phone from her pocket. "We're almost there. I need to call my mom," she said.

Black nodded. He heard the phone ring as Chasity held it to her ear. After a few rings, a deep voice jumped on the line.

"Balls residence," Black made out.

Chasity turned toward her window. "Hi, Ryan," she said.

The voice on the other side of the phone said something, but it was too faint for Black to understand.

"No, not really," Chasity continued. "I'm okay. I just need

to talk with mom. Is she around?" After listening to Ryan's reply, she said, "Yeah, I know, but she changed her cell number." Then she said, "Okay, I'll wait." She peeked over her shoulder at Black before continuing her phone conversation. "What is she doing in there? Okay. Oh, a meeting? Well, this is very important. Right. Did she say how soon before she can call back? Okay, well, I'm on my way there now. Alright. I'll see you soon. Bye." She ended the call and looked at Black. "That was my stepfather. My mom is home but in her office working and apparently can't be disturbed. Typical. Turn here."

Black made a right and drove a quarter of a mile before reaching a security hut. He stopped at the lift arm barrier and waited as a chubby guard exited the hut and walked over. Black rolled down his window. The guard bent down to look inside. His eyes widened when he saw Chasity.

"Hi Chasity, I haven't seen you in a while," he said, smiling and exposing the gap between his two front teeth.

"Hi Dennis," she said, returning the smile. "I'm here to see my mom. They're expecting me."

Dennis looked at Black as if he had just noticed him sitting at the wheel. "And who's this?" he asked.

"Oh, this is my new—bodyguard," she answered, her smile growing bigger.

The guard shifted his gaze between Black and Chasity for a moment. "Okay," he finally said, hunching his shoulders and walking back to the security hut.

Black looked at Chasity. "Old boyfriend?"

She winced at him. "Not on your nelly," she said, shaking her head.

Seconds later, the barrier lifted until it was vertical, and Black drove through as Chasity returned a goodbye wave to Dennis.

Black grinned at her gesture.

"Shut up," she said. "It's not like that."

They continued into the community, where various species and heights of palm trees welcomed them. Most of the homes hid behind high gates, but those visible had flush green lawns with four-car-garages.

"Pleasant neighborhood," Black said. "You grew up here?"

Chasity shook her head. "No, not at all. I grew up middle class in the UK. My father made sure we were always taken care of, but we never lived in places like this until after my music career took off," she said, staring at the windshield with dull eyes.

Black glanced at her before looking back at the road.

They drove another three minutes before Chasity instructed him to make a right turn onto a brick driveway. They passed through an open gate, and on the other side was a large, two-story, natural-stone veneer home. The grass and surrounding scrubs were a vibrant green. Enormous sycamore trees flanked either end of the house, and near the front door were two small palms. Black coasted up the semi-circle driveway, and Chasity motioned for him to park near the front door. The two exited the car in time to catch a cool breeze carrying the smell of fresh grass.

Chasity walked to the front door, and Black trailed a few paces behind. She rang the bell and took in a deep breath before exhaling slowly.

Footsteps approached from the other side, and the door swayed open. Standing behind it was a moderately-built man with short hair swept to the side and a salt-and-pepper goatee to match. He looked directly at Chasity, smiled, and embraced her.

"It's so good to see you, sweetheart," he said.

She hugged him back. "You too," she said with a quivering smile.

The man stepped back with her still in his arms. "Are you okay?" he asked. "You sounded worried over the phone."

Chasity pursed her lips and lowered her eyes, nodding for a moment. "I just need to talk to mom," she finally said.

The man looked at Black. "Who's this?" he asked, releasing Chasity and pivoting toward him.

"Oh, he's my bodyguard," she said, cutting her eyes at Black and smiling.

"Ryan Ball," the man said, walking to Black and extending his hand.

Black shook his hand, "Orlando Black."

"Nice to meet you, Mr. Black."

"Likewise."

"Well, let's get inside."

The trio entered into a large bright foyer. In front of them were a grand double staircase and a crystal chandelier hanging centered from above. They continued between the staircase and passed a room with the door cracked open. A woman's voice flowed from the room.

"I didn't tell you to do that. You need to learn to follow directions," the voice said in a low but stern tone.

"Oh, mom is still in her office," Chasity said, turning toward the room.

"Yes, but she'll meet us in here once she's done with her call," Ryan said, pointing to an open sitting room.

The space had a prominent vanilla scent. It was cozy but busy with bulky furniture. There was a hardwood coffee table in the middle with a long-skirted sofa and four skirted chairs surrounding it.

Ryan settled in one chair as Chasity circled the coffee table and sat on the couch. Black remained standing, observing the decor and pictures on the wall.

Chasity noticed. "Black. You can sit next to me," she said, smiling as she patted the seat cushion next to her.

He nodded and took a step toward the sofa but heard heels clicking behind him. He turned to find a woman wearing a black, draped-sleeve, sheath dress with matching high heels. She was fit but curvy. Her eyes were green, and her hair was burgundy with thin strips of gray throughout. She walked into the room and glanced at Ryan before fixing on Chasity.

"It's been a while, daughter," she said.

"Hello, mother," Chasity said, rolling her eyes.

The woman stared at her for a moment before scoffing and looking at Black.

"Who are you?" she asked through squinted eyes.

"That's Mr. Black," Ryan answered quickly.

"Well, Mr. Black, I'm Alice Ball. I have to apologize—I'm confused why you're here."

Black said nothing.

"He's my new bodyguard," Chasity said.

Alice's eyes widened, and her mouth opened. "You're the bodyguard…" she said. "A—a bodyguard. Why do you need a bodyguard?" she asked, shaking her head and turning to Chasity.

"We need to talk."

"What about?" Alice asked, sitting in a chair and crossing her legs.

She looked at Black. "You can have a seat, Mr. Black."

"I've been sitting a lot today. I think I'll stand."

"Suit yourself," she said, placing her attention on Chasity. "So, what's going on?"

"I… I'm not sure," Chasity answered. "Have you heard from dad? Has anyone reached out to you?"

Alice gasped. "I haven't seen your father in a long time. What happened?"

Chasity's eyes became dull. "They got him," her voice cracked. "They got dad, and I have less than thirty-six hours to pay them," she said, weeping.

Alice exhaled, and both of her eyebrows rose.

Ryan jumped up, dodging around the coffee table as he

sat next to his stepdaughter and placed his arm around her. "Who has him?" he asked.

"I don't know," Chasity answered, sniffling and wiping her nose with the back of her hand.

Alice looked at the floor before looking at Chasity. "Are you going to pay them?" she asked.

"How much do they want?" Ryan asked.

Chasity glared at her mother. "Yes, mom. They're serious. They held us at gunpoint," she snarked.

"They did what!" her mother asked, mouth gaping and gaze falling.

"Hey, Black," Ryan said. "You're a bodyguard. I'm sure you dealt with similar situations. What do you think?"

Black looked at Chasity. "Maybe you should call the authorities," he said.

"No, no, no," Alice contested. "I know cops, and some can't be trusted. This is a delicate situation. So, we have to handle it delicately."

"Oh, because that's how you always handle situations," Chasity blurted.

"Excuse me?"

"You never cared about him."

"What do you mean? I was married to him."

"Yeah, and all married couples love each other."

"That's enough, young lady."

Chasity stood and clenched her fist. "I have to get out of here," she said, threading around the coffee table to Black. "Can you give me a ride home?"

Black shared his gaze between her and Alice. "Sure," he said.

"Okay, let's go."

The two started toward the front door.

"Wait!" Alice called after them.

Chasity turned to find her mother quickly approaching.

"Where are you going?"

"Home."

"Why don't you stay here? At least until all this blows over," Alice said, stepping closer to Chasity.

"I don't think it's a good idea for me to be here right now."

"But sweetheart, you will be safe until we figure—"

Chasity waved her mother off. "I have to go," she said, exiting through the front door.

Black was behind her. He had his hand on the outside of the door and was about to exit when Alice's voice addressed him.

"Make sure you do your job," she said.

Black turned to face her. "Excuse me?"

"I'm sure she's paying you well. Make sure you keep my daughter out of harm's way."

Black's eyebrows rose, but he said nothing.

"Your primary focus should be to keep her away from all of this. I don't want her safety jeopardized because of a deadbeat."

"You mean her father."

Alice pointed her finger at Black. "You just keep her away from it and no cops," she asserted.

Black looked at her finger and then at her face. He squinted his eyes, the tension in his jaw visible. It was a hard stare that lasted a few seconds.

Alice looked away briefly. "It will all blow over," she said in a soft tone before turning and walking to Ryan, who stood near the staircase.

Black continued to glare at Mrs. Ball as she walked back to the sitting room with her husband.

This woman must have lost her mind, he thought, stepping outside and shutting the door upon his exit. He met Chasity standing at the car.

"What took so long?" she asked.

Black shook his head. "Nothing."

"Okay, let's go. I'm ready to get out of here."

BLACK SPENT THE first five minutes of the drive, trying to encourage Chasity to say more. Up to that point, she only gave him directions.

"So, what happened between you and your mom?" he finally asked.

Chasity folded her arms. "It's complicated."

"Well, make it simple."

"Maybe later," she sighed.

Black shrugged, placing his focus on the road.

"I'm sorry, Black," Chasity said, unfolding her arms. "It's like I've lost both of my parents, and I feel so alone."

"I know what you mean."

"You do?"

Black nodded. "When my parents passed away, it was lonely."

Chasity shifted in her seat to face him.

"But I'm thankful I had my sister and some great foster parents."

"I'm so sorry. I didn't know, Black."

"No need to be sorry."

"Do you ever talk to your foster parents?"

"Yes. As a matter of fact, I went to see them a few days ago."

"Well, it's good you stay in touch," Chasity said, forcing a smile.

"What about you? When was the last time you saw your father?"

"It's been a few years. But a few weeks back, I thought I saw someone who looked like him over in Hollywood. I mean… I hope it wasn't him."

"What do you mean?"

Her gaze dropped to the floor. "Th—the man I saw was

sitting on the pavement, resting against a building. He looked homeless. I glanced at him as I passed by on the sidewalk but didn't get a thorough look at him. I didn't… I was afraid to know if it was my father."

"But he looked like your father?" Black asked.

Chasity hunched her shoulders and shook her head at the same time. "I don't want to talk about it right now. Can we just enjoy the ride?" she said with gentle eyes.

Black glanced into her eyes and nodded.

"Good," she said, turning and looking out her window.

They drove another fifteen minutes in silence before she instructed him to make a left turn onto a road with a slight incline. The road snaked uphill for a mile, taking them to a three-story condominium-style home surrounded by a tall compound wall. Black stopped at the gated entrance while Chasity removed her smartphone. She poked at it for a few seconds before the gate slid open. He turned to her, giving her a *that's pretty slick* look.

She shrugged. "Smart home," she said.

Black nodded before pulling into the driveway and watched in his mirror as the gate slid closed. The house was a natural white, almost gray, and had a light brown trim. It had sharp angles and several large windows. There wasn't much of a yard, but the home's top floor had a large open patio area. As they continued up the short driveway to the garage door, Chasity pressed at her phone again. The garage door rolled up, and they drove inside as the ceiling LED lights flicked on. The large space housed a black Porsche Cayenne, a red Lamborghini, and one other vehicle that seemed out of place.

"What's up with the Toyota Prius?" Black asked, throwing his car into park.

Chasity chuckled. "I know, right?" she said. "But some-times you just want to go about your day unnoticed. Plus, that car is good on gas and good for the environment."

The two exited the Viper, and Black followed Chasity as she began walking toward a door to the main house. He browsed studying the Porsche and Lamborghini, and confirmed the garage door rolled closed before they stepped inside. The room they entered was an open foyer. It had a woodsy and earthy scent. A flight of stairs stood in front of them, and to their left, a narrow hallway leading to what appeared to be a bathroom.

They took the stairs to the second floor, which was a spacious living area. The kitchen flowed into the dining room, which opened into a modern furnished living area. Dark hardwood covered the entire floor, and the large windows extended light to every inch of the space.

"Can I get you anything?" Chasity asked, pointing toward the kitchen.

Black shook his head. "I'm okay for now. Thanks."

They continued into the living area.

"Make yourself at home," Chasity said as she plopped onto a large couch.

Black observed the various awards on the walls and shelves before taking a seat next to her. She had already relaxed into the cushion and closed her eyes. He said nothing, just glanced at her briefly, and continued looking around the house.

"I'm not sleeping," Chasity said. "Just resting my eyes."

"You look tired."

"I am. There's always something going on."

"Maybe you should take a vacation when all of this is over."

"Yeah, right. I don't remember the last time I've taken a holiday."

"That's exactly my point."

She looked at him, smiling and eyes half shut. "If I go on vacation, will you come with me?"

"You want to take me? I figured you'd go with Bridget."

Chasity opened her eyes fully and adjusted on the couch. "Oh yeah. I should probably try calling her again," she said before staring at Black.

They momentarily fixed on each other.

She slowly batted her eyes. "But that's not what I meant. On my next vacation, I'd prefer the company of a man. That's why I asked you."

"I'm sure you have a boyfriend," he said, with a grin on his face. "You strike me as the dirty blond type."

Chasity rolled her eyes and scoffed. "You've been watching the news?" she said. "That dirty blond is Calvin, and he's my ex."

"Did you two split on good terms?"

"I guess you could say that. It felt pretty mutual. We just didn't gel well, but what's interesting is my mother was very fond of him. The two of them had a lot in common."

"How do you mean?"

"I don't... his family is wealthy. He's kind of—" Chasity struggled for words. "How can I explain it? I know. I'll start with my mother. Her parents, my grandparents, always did well for themselves, so she never lacked as a child."

"Nothing wrong with that."

"I know, but my father always had a good job, so again she always had what she needed. And then, when my career took off, she had all she would ever need."

"So, your mother never worked."

"Exactly. Other than being my manager, she never held a job for very long. Never created anything for herself. She's only—family famous, you know?"

Black nodded.

"That's what I mean. Calvin is the same way, and I just can't deal with that kind of energy."

"Is that why your mom is no longer your manager?"

Chasity exhaled. "Yeah, that's definitely part of it."

"What's the other part?"

"Let's just say—"

"Irreconcilable differences," Black finished her sentence.

Chasity ogled him. "You're a troublemaker."

Black shrugged. "No, but it knows how to find me."

She stared at him for a few seconds more before standing from the couch. "I have some phone calls I need to make, and I'm going to go wash up. Do you need anything?"

He shook his head, relaxing into the couch.

"Okay, but don't think about leaving. I'm setting the alarm; you're trapped now," she said, smiling and pressing at her phone.

He watched her from behind as she walked in the kitchen's direction. Thoughts about her from his subconscious came forward. She had a fit, hourglass shape and an alluring stride, he thought as she disappeared down a hall behind the kitchen.

Black closed his eyes, figuring he'd take an early afternoon nap just in case he was in for a long night.

HIS EYES OPENED to the sound of dishes clinking and the smell of stir-fry. He looked and saw Chasity in the kitchen near the stove. She had her hair tied back and wore workout leggings with a matching sports bra.

Chasity noticed him. "Look who's awake. Did you enjoy your little nap?"

Black stood and stretched. "It was okay," he said, yawning, then walking to the kitchen. "How long was I out?"

"Not long. About an hour," she answered, pouring sauce into a wok and shaking it.

"I thought you'd have a cook."

"Not today. I like to do things for myself sometimes."

"It smells good."

"Thanks. It's almost ready. Here," she said, handing him a couple of plates with silverware on top. "Go set the table."

In the dining room, there was a square table that sat four. He set the plates across from each other and walked back into the kitchen.

"Anything else?" he asked.

She nodded at two cups and some napkins on the kitchen counter. "Only the lemonade and napkins, please. It's ready."

Black walked to the table and set the cups and napkins down. On his way back into the kitchen to wash his hands, he passed Chasity, who was carrying two serving plates. One had rice on it, and the other had stir fry chicken with vegetables. He washed his hands and met her at the table. They sat and began scooping rice and stir-fry onto their plates.

"So, have you decided what you're going to do?" Black asked.

Chasity sighed at the question. "Yeah, I have no choice but to pay them. While you were napping, I called my accountant and talked with him about getting the money. I didn't tell him what it was for, although he asked a lot of questions. He assured me he could have it all together before tomorrow morning."

"Were you able to reach Bridget?"

"I called but still didn't get her, and my mom called me like five times, but I didn't answer."

Black said nothing.

Chasity reached across the table and touched his hand. "Hey, let's just enjoy our lunch."

They briefly smiled at each other before moving their attention to their meals. Between chewing their food and drinking their lemonade, they had discussions about what their plans were once everything was over. Chasity did most of the talking. She mentioned an album she was finishing and a trip to Japan she was planning. Black didn't have any plans. The only thing he could share was that he would head east.

"That was great," he said, pushing his plate away.

"Good. I'm happy you enjoyed it."

He gripped his plate and reached for Chasity's empty plate.

"No, I got it," she said, quickly grabbing both plates. "You're a guest, and you did enough already helping set-up. I'll clean up," she finished, standing and walking toward the sink.

A buzz followed by a musical tone flowed from the kitchen. Chasity gasped, and Black looked in the sound's direction, noticing two phones on the counter. He recognized one as Chasity's smartphone, and the other was the flip phone the kidnappers gave her.

She settled the plates in the sink and scrambled to the phones, extending her hand and snatching the smartphone off the countertop.

"Thank you," she exhaled, glancing at the phone's screen and holding it to her ear. "Where are you? I've been trying to reach you."

Black stood and walked to her, stopping a couple of steps behind.

"So, you're okay?" Chasity asked into the phone. "Okay, great. Yeah, I know—you won't believe what happened."

Before she could utter her next syllable, another buzz vibrated throughout the kitchen. It was like the first but different in rhythm. Between the rings, the room was completely silent.

Both Black and Chasity stared at the flip phone as it shook on the counter.

"I… I have to call you back, Bridget," Chasity said, ending the call.

She looked at Black before picking up the flip phone and exhaling. "Hel—Hello," she answered. "Yes, I'll have it by tomorrow morn—what? You said—no wait, please—"

Chasity's hand dropped from her ear, and her mouth fell open.

"What did they say?" Black asked.

"They—I. Black…" she shook her head. "They said—they said I have four hours to get them the money," she finally blurted. Tears formed in her eyes. "I don't know what I'm going to do."

Black took in a breath and exhaled, shaking his head in thought. "Something's wrong. Really wrong," he said, gently laying his hands on her shoulders. "I have something I need to ask, but I need you to give it some thought before answering, okay?"

She nodded, wiping the tears from her eyes and the sniffle from her nose.

"Do you have someone you trust? I mean, you really trust?"

Chasity nodded again. "Yes. Bridget."

"Do you really trust her?"

"Absolutely."

Black removed his hands from her shoulders. "Okay, pack some clothes. I want the two of you to get out of town."

"What about my father?"

"I don't think… Look, something is off, and you need to keep yourself safe."

"My father may not be perfect, but I can't abandon him."

"You're not abandoning him. Just making yourself harder to find."

"If I do as they say, everything should be fine."

"They're criminals. They can't be trusted. Remember, you had thirty-six hours, now you only have four? That's what people like this do—they lie."

Chasity whimpered.

"It may not be safe here. I need you to call your friend and get out of town now."

She nodded. "You may be right," she said before walking out of the kitchen, leaving both the phones on the counter.

Black watched her pace down the hall and out of his sight. The sound of a door opening and closing followed seconds after.

Chasity's smartphone lit up a blue hue. Black picked it up and noticed it was still unlocked. A notification for a missed call from 'Mother' displayed on the screen. He clicked it, and the phone's recent calls displayed. There were seven missed calls from that number. The voicemail symbol showed two unheard messages, both from 'Mother.' The first was nearly two hours prior, and the second was within the last hour. He tapped the first message and held the phone to his ear as Alice Ball's voice sounded.

"Young lady, you're being unreasonable. Why not just come back here until we figure out how we're going to handle this? Call me back."

Black pressed the second message before moving the phone back to his ear, and Alice's voice started again.

"Chasity, sweetheart, please call me back. We really need to talk. It's imperative you call me."

The message ran in silence for a few more seconds before ending, and Black looked at the screen, cuffing his chin. As he placed the phone on the counter, it rang, displaying a picture of a face he had seen before. He pressed the answer button. Holding the phone to his ear, he immediately heard a car door closing and an engine start.

"Chas?" Bridget's voice called, followed by heavy drums and loud guitar chords, no doubt from the car's radio.

The volume quickly dropped, and the line went silent for a beat.

"I'm sorry about that," she said. "Where are you?"

"She's in the back, packing," Black answered.

"Who's this? Where's Chasity?"

"I'm a friend—her bodyguard."

"Where's Chasity?" she asked again.

"Like I said, she's in the back."

"I don't know who you are, but Chasity doesn't have a personal bodyguard."

"Your name is Bridget, right?"

"Yes. How do you know?"

"She told me. Look, she'll call you back soon," Black said, ending the call.

He patted the phone against his palm and swayed his head from side to side before finally placing the phone on the counter.

A few minutes later, Chasity returned with a small duffel bag. She had covered her sports bra with a zipped hoodie. By that time, Black was back in the living room, sitting on the couch.

"I'm ready to go," she said, allowing a hint of sadness into her voice.

"Okay, good. Bridget called. I told her you'll call her back."

Chasity squinted. "You answered my phone?" she asked in a tone that was neither accepting nor disapproving but something in between.

Black shrugged at the question. "Never mind that. You two need to leave town. Someplace no one knows about."

"You're coming with us, right?"

He didn't answer. Just looked at her and sighed.

"You're not coming," Chasity said, her gaze falling to the floor.

Black stood and walked to her. "Everything will work out," he said, holding her shoulders.

She gently pulled away from him. "How can you be so sure?"

He said nothing. Mainly because he didn't have enough information to be a hundred percent sure, only a hunch.

"I have a question," he deflected. "You mentioned your mother never really had to take care of herself. I'm curious to know what your stepfather does for a living?"

Chasity squinted with a slight frown. "Good question. He was in banking, but I don't think he's doing much now, outside of small investments. I think he has a small nest egg. Living off that, I guess."

"He doesn't strike me as a flashy guy."

"No. He's really not at all," she said, dropping her duffel bag on the floor. "I'm going to call Bridget," she finished before walking into the kitchen and grabbing her phone. She jabbed at the screen and held the phone to her face before strolling to where Black stood.

"Hi Bridget," she said. "No, no, no, I'm fine. He kind of is. But where have you been? I called you a dozen times."

There was a long moment of silence before Chasity nodded. "Okay—well, whatever. It's okay. It's okay. Look, there is something very serious happening, and I need you to go out of town with me. I'll—yes… I'll explain it all later. Could you pack a bag and meet me at our favorite shoe store?" she asked, her voice cracking. "Okay. See you soon. Bye."

"You okay?" Black asked.

"Yes," she said, brushing across her nose with the back-side of her hand.

"Did Bridget mention where she's been for the past few hours?"

"Huh? Oh yeah, she mentioned she went looking for me, and her phone died."

"Right."

"Well, I better go meet her," Chasity said, pursing her lips before continuing. "You sure you don't want to come?" she asked, her voice cracking again.

He was quiet for a moment. "Yeah, I think I'll tag along," he said, smiling.

She briefly closed her eyes before opening them with a wide smile.

"Let's get out of here. I'll drive," he said.

• • •

THEY TOOK THE Viper, stopping only once to gas up the car before arriving at the shoe store. It was a large warehouse building among other shopping outlets and restaurants in a fairly populous area with moderate foot traffic.

Black found a parking spot near the back of the lot. Both he and Chasity exited the car and walked toward the shopping center. The entire time, Chasity was on the phone with Bridget receiving directions to her location.

She sat at a circular umbrella table outside a sandwich shop next to the shoe store. When she saw them approaching, she jumped from her seat and threaded between the tables and chairs toward Chasity.

"Chas, I'm so sorry," she said, hugging her. "What's going on?"

Chasity hugged her back but didn't answer the question. The two released their embrace.

Bridget looked at Black. "Are you the bodyguard?" she asked.

"Yeah, something like that," he said.

"What do you mean? What's going on?"

"Let's sit for a few minutes. I'll explain," Chasity said.

Bridget took her original seat, and Chasity sat next to her. Black remained standing, surveying the area for any threats. There were none, so he sat in a chair on the other side of Bridget.

It took Chasity six and a half minutes to tell her friend about the kidnappers, her abducted father, what they want in exchange for him, and her plan to get out of town.

"So, they said you had thirty-six hours, but then they changed it to four?" Bridget whispered. "That's really bizarre."

"It's so unfair," Chasity said.

"Yeah, but it tells us something about them you can use to your advantage," Black said.

"What?"

"They're in a hurry."

"Which means?"

"It means they need this money, and they're going to keep making mistakes."

Chasity hunched her shoulder. "I don't understand. How can you be sure?" she asked, shaking her head.

"Because of how quick and drastically the timetable changed. If they felt you could've delivered the money within eight hours, why not give you that deadline, to begin with? Something happened. Something has them spooked."

Bridget was quiet.

Chasity rested her cheek on the knuckles of her hand and wrinkled her forehead. Seconds later, she lifted her head with a comment.

"It's refreshing to hear something now has them worried, and they're starting to make mistakes."

"They've been making mistakes the whole time. Do you think they meant to take me along with you? No. They wanted to get to you badly and got impatient. I was just along for the ride. I suppose they would've grabbed anyone who was with you at the time. They wanted you quickly. They wanted the money quickly."

"Why take you from there?" Bridget chimed in. "How did they know where you were?"

Black said nothing.

"I don't know, but why me?" Chasity said. "If they need money, why not just go rob a bank or something?"

"They felt getting the money from you would be easier," Black said.

"But why would they feel that way?" Bridget asked.

"Yeah, why?" Chasity echoed the question.

Black shrugged. "My guess, someone who's close enough to you convinced them," he answered.

The table went silent.

"We should get going," he said.

Within five minutes, they were on I-405 North. Black and Chasity were in the Viper, and Bridget drove behind them in a silver BMW.

Black checked the rearview mirror to make sure she wasn't falling behind.

Chasity noticed. "Is Bridget okay back there?"

He nodded. "I think so."

"Good. Just so you know, we're going to be on this road for a while," she said, pointing at the windshield. "I'm going to call my accountant," she added.

Black shrugged, already knowing why she wanted to make the call.

She spent a quarter of an hour going back and forth with the man on the phone.

"Okay, fine. Just let me know when you have it," she finally ended the call and made a heavy exhale.

Black glanced at her. "Let me guess. He can't get that type of money together in only a few hours," he said before swinging his sights back on the road.

"I don't know what I'm going to do."

"It will be okay."

"You keep saying that, and I hope you're right, but do you really know for sure?"

He didn't answer, just gazed out at the road.

"Oh, I need to make another call."

"Who are you calling this time?"

"My lawyer."

He looked at her with a raised brow.

"I talked with her earlier when you were napping at my house. She told me not to tell anyone, but I gave her a brief description of the kidnappers, and she's looking into them."

"How much you think she can do with brief descriptions?"

"Probably a lot—she's fantastic at what she does. Very

smart—kind of like you in that sense. Not to mention she has lots of connections."

"She sounds expensive."

"Yep, and worth every dime. I'm sure all of her clients would tell you the same."

"So, what advice did she give you about your father?"

Chasity didn't answer immediately. Her eyes wandered as if she was hoping the question would fade away.

"What? You don't remember?" Black pressed.

"Yes. Of course, I remember. She wanted to talk with the kidnappers and attempt to negotiate before trying anything else."

"That sounds like the lawyer thing to do."

"Yeah, but I was afraid they'd hurt my father if I let her do that. But now I wish I'd let her try."

"It'll be okay."

"That's your favorite thing to say, huh?" she said, smiling.

She continued smiling at him for a moment before making the call. The phone conversation was brief. Only three minutes passed before Chasity ended the call.

"That was quick. I'm guessing your lawyer doesn't have anything yet."

"She has something but wanted to confirm before sharing it with me. She said she'll call back soon."

Black looked in his rearview mirror and saw Bridget's mouth moving. Her forehead wrinkled, and her eyes were as wide as the lens of her glasses. She appeared to be shouting at the dash of her car. He made a mental note of it, placing his attention back on the road and watching as the palm trees and buildings rolled past.

Dry dunes and small mountains soon replaced the trees and buildings. They drove another hour before exiting the highway onto a narrow, two-lane road that zigged and zagged for a few miles, surrounded by various pine, cedar, and oak trees.

"I love this forest," Chasity commented.

"You come here a lot?" Black asked.

She shook her head, "Not as often as I'd like."

"Just to be sure—who all knows about this place?"

"Me, Bridget, and now you," she answered, pursing her lips as she concluded.

Black looked into his mirror and saw Bridget about a car's length behind. She was staring straight and massaging her upper lip with her bottom set of teeth.

"Make a right here," Chasity instructed.

He flicked on his indicator and eased the car onto a dirt road. There was forestry on either side, but the road was well-maintained. The path was clear and defined as if the owner regularly laid dirt and edged, but the ride was still bumpy. Half a mile up the road, a sign welcomed them to the Paradise Springs Cabin Resort, and the bumps under the car smoothed out as the road changed from dirt to asphalt. A large, log building with a parking lot came into sight on the left.

Black slowed the car. Bridget, still trailing close behind, did the same.

"You can keep going," Chasity said. "That's the main office—the welcome center. I own the cabin we're staying in, so we're good."

They continued along the road, passing a few log cabin apartments, a playground, some picnic areas, a few single cabin homes, and a restaurant. Guests were outside talking and playing, while others were packing up or unloading their vehicles. This activity continued throughout the community until they reached a small lake. Other than a boat and a couple of people fishing, pedestrian traffic was minimum.

They circled the lake until Chasity gave directions to make a right turn onto a gravel road. The Viper's tires crunched across the rocks for fifty yards, bringing them to a contemporary designed cabin. Moderately sized, it sat alone but not deep in the woods. Black noted the large windows and a patio area with an outdoor fire pit.

"This is it," she said.

Black stopped the car, jolting the gear in park. He delayed exiting the vehicle to inspect the area around the property.

"So, what do you think?" she asked.

"Is this the only road in? Those windows are large."

"Yes. And the windows have working shutters."

They left the car and stretched, then walked to the front door. Black stood a few paces behind Chasity, surveying the outside of the cabin, making a note of the number twelve imprinted above the door while she fetched her key and fiddled with the lock.

Bridget made her way over just as the door clicked open, and the three entered. Chasity stepped inside first with Bridget, then Black followed.

The inside was spacious and full of natural light. The smell of oak and lavender permeated the entranceway, and beyond the small foyer was an open living area connecting to a kitchen furnished with modern appliances and an island.

Black immediately noticed the kitchen had a door leading outside.

Chasity walked into the living room and performed a spin while lifting her hands in the air. "Home away from home," she said before pointing to a hall in the back. "There are only two bedrooms, so—"

"I'll take the couch," Black said.

"Are you sure? I was about to say Bridget and I could share a room."

"It's okay. I'll be fine in here."

Chasity shrugged. "Alright then," she said, walking into the kitchen with Bridget tailing her.

Black walked down the hall where he found two identical rooms, one on the right and the other on the left. A bed, dresser drawer, and desk were all that occupied them. The room on the left was larger, and the room on the right had a door leading to the patio in the back. Further down the hall, near the end, was a bathroom. He heard laughter coming from the living area. When he walked back, he saw the two young women snickering with their hands over their mouths. Both seemed oblivious that he watched them. The two appeared to be having fun. They seemed happy. But the mood slowly changed.

Chasity's giggle slowly transformed into a whimper. Then a sob. And finally, a bawl.

Bridget embraced her friend, whispering calming words and rubbing her back.

Black ducked into the hall and went to the bathroom, figuring it would give Chasity enough time to deal with her emotions. When he returned, he peeked around the corner and saw the women sitting on the couch.

Chasity was at the edge facing Bridget, which also put her line of sight in Black's direction. She was speaking to Bridget, but too softly for him to hear. Reading her lips, he could make out some phrasing. *What am I going to do...* and *this is all my fault...* were the most repeated. And between every couple of breaths, she would use her index figures to wipe under her watery eyes.

Bridget sat reclined with her elbow resting on top of the back pillow and her hand palming the side of her head. She used her free hand to rub Chasity's shoulder.

Black waited for the emotional debris to clear the air before stepping into the living room and walking to them.

Bridget turned, looking at him over the back of the couch.

Chasity brushed her fingers across her eyes before forcing a smile at him. "Hi," she said.

"I'll get the bags from the car," he told her.

She nodded, still smiling at him.

The moment he stepped outside, he felt the cool, late afternoon breeze across his face, shifting the leaves on the ground as it passed.

He looked up, hoping to see the sky, but there were only spots of blue beyond the foliage canopying above him. The birds' soft chirps helped him relax in his thoughts. He thought Chasity was safe. That she had some support and would be all right. Then the thought to leave her bag at the door, hop in his car, and drive to Vegas crossed his mind. But another thought hit him as a shaft of sunlight made its way through the trees and to his eyes. She had asked him *how could he be so sure everything would work out?* It bothered him because he was only ninety-five percent sure everything would work out, and that extra five percent was enough to get someone killed. He decided he'd see it through until she and her father were safe.

When he returned inside the house, he found Chasity and Bridget now stood at the kitchen island.

"There he is," Bridget said.

"What took so long?" Chasity asked.

Black shrugged at the question, laying two small bags on the floor near the door.

"We're thinking of grabbing a bite to eat. There's a restaurant near the main resort area."

"Okay. Let's go. It'll be dark soon."

"We can take my car," Bridget offered.

They made sure all the doors and windows were locked and walked outside. The two women made their way to Bridget's car, and Black was behind them but stopped at his car.

Chasity didn't notice Black had stopped following until she opened the door of Bridget's car. "Hey, are you coming?" she asked.

"Yeah, I'll follow you guys," he said.

She hunched her shoulders and eased into the front passenger seat. Bridget looked at her, and the two exchanged a few words before the engine turned over.

Black slid into the Viper and followed them.

The restaurant adhered to the same theme as most of the other buildings in the resort. It was an extensive structure made of log with a porch running the length of its front. The parking lot was mostly vacant, making it easy to find a spot near the entrance.

Black met Chasity and Bridget near the front of the restaurant, and they entered together. They passed through a gift shop filled with clothes, toys, cookware, and snacks. On the other side of the shop, the aroma of grilled steak with a hint of sauteed carrots and fresh-baked bread stuffed the area.

They stood at the hostess station for less than a minute before a waitress approached and escorted them to a table. They sat and began a light-hearted conversation. Chasity and Bridget did most of the talking, while Black mainly listened. There was talk about Chasity's new album and some memories she had of the resort. The conversation shifted to how she and Bridget met and where they planned to travel. There were a lot of smiles and laughter at the table. It was as if everyone agreed to ignore the negative circumstances just long enough to enjoy dinner and each other's company. Thirty-five minutes later, they were clearing their plates, and the waitress made her way over.

"How was everything?" she asked.

"Delicious," Chasity said with a smile.

"Will this be separate checks?"

"No, it's all one check."

The server grabbed their plates and walked toward the kitchen.

Black looked at Chasity, who wore a smile. "Thanks," he said.

"Yeah, it was good, Chas," Bridget added.

"No. Thank you," she said, looking at Black, maintaining her smile.

She glanced at the screen of her phone, and the smile on her face slowly arched in the opposite direction.

Black kept his eyes on her. Maybe the reality of her situation suddenly came back to her. Maybe she felt guilty because she was enjoying herself while her father was in trouble. Maybe she was feeling hopeless.

She met Black's eyes with her own. "There's just a little over an hour before I'm supposed to have the money," she said, pursing her lips.

Black said nothing.

"Don't worry, Chas. We'll figu—" Bridget started saying before her phone rang. She looked at the screen for a moment and bit her lip. It was a microexpression, quick, but Black caught it. "I have to take this," she said, standing and walking toward the gift shop.

Black watched her until she disappeared into the shop. When he moved his attention back to Chasity, he saw her staring into space.

"What did you say the title of your new album is?" he asked, attempting to move her thoughts to something more positive.

She tilted her head and grinned as if she knew what he was trying to do and was thanking him for it. "Why?" she asked.

"I was thinking about getting a copy."

"Yeah, right. There's only been one man close to me who listened to my music."

"Who? Your ex?"

"Please. Calvin's into heavy rock. I meant my father."

"Wait. So, your ex likes rock music?"

"Yes."

"Does Bridget?"

"No way. She's into smooth R&B."

Black looked in the direction of the gift shop. "You don't say."

"Yeah. I have nothing against it, just not what I do."

The waitress came and dropped off the check. Black reached for his wallet, but Chasity waved him off.

"I got it," she said.

"Habit," he said, shrugging.

She placed a hundred-dollar bill on top of the check and opened her mouth to speak but shifted her attention to Bridget returning to the table.

"Is everything okay?" Chasity asked her.

"Yeah," Bridget sighed. "Nothing to worry about."

Black kept his eyes on her as she sat and touched Chasity's hand.

"We'll get through it," she said.

MOMENTS LATER THEY stood outside of the restaurant. The sun was starting its descent, and the air breezed with a slight chill. They drove back to the cabin, where Black inspected the inside. He started in the living quarters and ended with the back rooms. There was nothing unusual. Nothing out of place. Everything was as they had left it. He returned to the living area and found the two women sitting on the couch. Chasity leaned forward with her face in her palms, and Bridget rubbed her friend's back. The two looked up as they saw him approach.

"I'm going to the front office. I'll be back soon," he said to Chasity.

She said nothing, only looked at him with puffy eyes, and nodded.

"Don't worry. I won't let anything happen to you."

"I know," she said, a crackle in her voice. "I'm more concerned about my father," she said, sobbing.

Bridget hugged her. "It's going to be okay," she said.

Black turned away and walked to the door. As he reached for the doorknob, he heard Bridget's voice.

"They're supposed to call in an hour," she said.

"I know," he replied, with his back to them. "I won't be long."

Within five minutes, he parked at the main office. He walked inside, and a skinny kid with freckles greeted him. The smooth-skinned young man stood at a desk placed in front of a wall with the words *Welcome Center* written on it.

"Can I help you, sir?" the kid asked.

"Is there a manager here?"

"Yes, sir," he said, pointing to a dark-bearded man at a counter near the back of the office.

"Thanks."

"My pleasure," the kid said, shuffling some papers on his desk as if he was getting ready to leave for the day.

Black walked across the carpet, which quickly turned into tile, passing a brick fireplace with three rocking chairs surrounding it and brushing by an older, married couple before reaching the counter.

"Hi, sir. How can I help you?" the bearded man asked.

"I was planning on walking some trails in the woods, but I'm concerned about aggressive animals. Is there a park ranger of some type of law enforcement around?"

"Well—we have a park ranger, but he's not always available."

"No type of law enforcement available?"

"Nothing like cops. We do have security that patrols the community. But if you're worried about being attacked by an animal, I can assure you that's not likely to happen. I can't think of a single case of someone being attacked by an animal —and I've been here twelve years."

"I see. So, you guys probably don't have paramedics on-site either?"

"We have a couple of medics on-site for minor things, but for large emergencies, we recommend calling nine-one-one.

The cops, fire department, and paramedics are close by and can be here in less than fifteen minutes."

Black nodded.

"But if you're concerned about the animals, I suggest not walking the trails at night and always take someone with you."

"Okay, thanks."

"Pleasure, sir. Enjoy the rest of your day," the man concluded.

Black walked outside and looked at his car. After thinking for a moment, he chose to walk back to the cabin staying close to the left side of the road the entire way, observing as people cleared out of the picnic areas and the road increased with traffic heading toward the front of the community. The sun sparked its last rays of light, and duskiness overcame the area by the time he made it to the cabin. He noticed the window shutters were closed, and a light gleamed from around the back of the cabin. His instincts kicked in, and he swiveled his head, looking for anything out of place as he crept toward the house but found nothing. The outside light above the front door flickered on at the same time he reached for the handle.

The door swung open, and Bridget was on the other side. "Hey. We saw you walking up," she said. "Wasn't sure if it was you at first."

Black made no verbal reply. *Well, at least they're on alert*, he thought, stepping inside and locking the door.

Bridget walked to the couch where Chasity sat. It didn't look like they moved much since he left. He joined them in the living room, sitting in a chair close to Chasity's side of the couch.

She looked at him. "Thirty minutes," she said.

"I know. Did you ever call your mother back?" he asked.

She winced. "No. And I don't plan on calling her."

The moment Chasity completed her sentence, a phone

rang. She jumped from the couch and reached into her pocket, removing her smartphone.

"Hi," she spoke into the phone.

Black stood. "Speaker," he whispered to her.

She looked at him and nodded. "Hey, is it okay if I put you on speaker?" Chasity listened for a beat. "My best friend and my bodyguard," she said.

It was clear she was giving careful consideration to what was being said. She shared a stare between Black and Bridget before inhaling. "Yes, I do," she said, exhaling at the end.

The person on the other side of the phone said something else, and Chasity waved Black and Bridget to the kitchen's island before pressing at her phone screen. She placed the phone on top of the island, and the three crowded around.

"Okay, we're listening," Chasity said.

A woman's voice rose from the speakers. "Hello everyone. My name is Sandra Keyes, and I'm Chasity's lawyer," she said. "I know we're short on time, so I'll get right into it. The two Latinos you described to me, Chasity, the woman Eva Larez, and the man Lucas Ortega—are associated with the Zarate cartel."

"The cartel," Bridget echoed.

"Yeah."

"So, the cartel's behind this?" Chasity asked.

"Not necessarily," Sandra said. "I made some calls and did some digging. Apparently, Larez and Ortega are no longer in the cartel."

"Do you know why?"

"From what I could find, the two started skimming money from the cartel. And as you can imagine, the cartel's drug lords and lieutenants would not let their actions go unpunished. Long story short, Larez and Ortega have been on the run for the past three months."

Chasity sighed. "What does any of this have to do with me?"

"You're a job," Black said.

"I'm sorry, are you the bodyguard?" Sandra asked.

"Yes."

"What's your name?"

"Let's stick with bodyguard for now."

"Fair enough," she said with a chuckle. "Chasity, Mr. Bodyguard is right. They're probably trying to make a quick buck off you so they can continue to fund their escape from the cartel."

"This makes no sense. Why me—why would they choose me?" Chasity said, hunching her shoulders and swinging her gaze between Black and Bridget.

"You're an easy job," Black said. "Or at least that's how it was sold to them."

"Sold to them by who?"

"Whoever hired them."

"And who's that?"

Black said nothing.

"That's the game-winning question," Sandra said.

Silence. No one said anything for a good ten seconds.

Black was the first to break the silence. "What about the other guy?" he asked, craning over the phone.

"The other guy?" Sandra repeated.

"The cop who was with them."

"Wait," Chasity interrupted. "How do you know he's a cop?"

"The way he held his gun. And the way he walked and talked. You see it enough times you can spot them a mile away."

"His name is Phillip Kidman," Sandra stated. "And you're right, Mr. Bodyguard, he is a cop. I was still looking into him, so I forgot to mention him, but I think I've already gathered enough to conclude his involvement."

"And what's that?"

"Well, I'll give you the facts, and you can tell me. I learned there is an internal affairs' investigation on him; his wife recently left him, and he's three months behind on his mortgage."

"Which means he's just in it for the money."

"That's my conclusion."

Bridget pushed her glasses up the bridge of her nose. "So, what are we going to do when they call?"

"Initially, I wanted to talk with them and strike some sort of deal," Sandra said. "But at the time, we weren't entirely sure of their motives. Now that we know more about who they are and what they want, I believe making a deal is definitely the best course of action. The problem is, negotiating with people like this requires prudence—they'll always try to gain the upper hand. On top of that, we only have one way to get in contact with them, and they're in control of when that happens. We're running short on time, and I won't be able to reach you quickly enough to have that conversation so—"

"I'll talk with them," Black cut in.

Chasity and Bridget both looked at him.

"Do you have any experience handling negotiations of this nature, Mr. Bodyguard?"

"A little."

"You seem very sharp, but that doesn't sound too convincing."

"It's like you said. We now know more about them and their motives—this gives us the upper hand. I'll just make sure they know that."

"What about my father?" Chasity asked.

Black stood straight and turned to her. "You're going to have to trust me on this," he said.

She nodded, exhaling as her gaze bounced from the floor to the kitchen island's countertop.

"I guess that's the plan for now," Sandra said. "Mr. Bodyguard, I'm counting on you. And Chasity, call me immediately after they call."

"Okay," Chasity said.

"Alright then, good luck, and I'll speak with you all soon."

"Before you go," Black said.

"Yes?"

"Ortega and Larez, what were their ranks in the cartel?"

"Larez was a lieutenant, and Ortega was a sicario."

Black glanced at Chasity. She had one ear turned to the phone and was squinting with her lips parted.

"Thanks," he said to Sandra.

"You got it. Remember, call me right after talking to them. I'll be waiting for your call."

"Okay, thank you," Chasity said.

"Anytime. Talk with you soon, bye."

The call ended.

Chasity picked up the phone and tapped at the screen. "What's a sicario?" she asked, directing the question at Black.

"It's muscle for the cartel," he said.

"You mean like a hitman?" Bridget asked.

"Yeah, something like that."

"Great," Chasity said. "That means he's killed before."

"Probably."

"This isn't good," she continued as she looked at her phone. "And less than sixteen minutes to go."

"Try not to get worked up."

"You don't understand," she raised her voice. "There're killers out there with my father," she said as she made her way toward the hall.

"Hey," he called to her. "Give me the flip phone," he extended his hand.

Chasity stopped and walked to him, placing the phone in his hand.

"It may be best if you're not around when I talk with them."

She exhaled and rolled her eyes before making her way to the hall.

Bridget went after her but stopped at Black first. "She was already dealing with a lot, so this is very difficult for her," she said, following her friend.

He watched as the two disappeared into the hall. Shortly after, the sound of a door slamming shut flowed from the hallway into the living quarters. He shook his head, tossing the phone in his hand before resting it in his pocket and finding a seat on the couch. A faint conversation soon drifted from the hall. No doubt a word or two was said about him, but it didn't bother his conscience in the least. After a couple of minutes, he felt agitated. He decided fresh air would help and used the kitchen door to the back patio. He walked to the edge of the deck, resting his arms on the railing and looking out into the evening forest gloom. Birds and crickets chirped at him as the glow from the outside patio light cast a shadow in front of him. He stayed that way for a few minutes until the outside patio door to the bedrooms caught his eye. He didn't hear any voices coming from the other side, so he was certain the girls were in the room on the opposite side of the hall. He shrugged at the thought and went back inside.

When he entered the kitchen, he felt a vibration in his pocket. He removed the phone and, when he flipped it open, saw *No Caller ID* at the top of the tiny screen.

"Yeah," he answered.

"Who's this?" a deep voice asked.

Black had heard the voice before and could put a name to it now, *Lucas Ortega*.

"I'm the one you'll be talking with."

"Oh," Ortega said, a chuckle in his voice. "This must be the bodyguard. I suggest you put that tramp on before something happens to her father."

"You're talking with me."

"Listen to me—" Ortega yelled.

"No, you listen," Black cut him off, snapping back even

louder. "If you want to see your money, you'll talk with me—and you're not getting a dime without providing some proof of life."

"You want proof of life," Ortega grunted. "I'll give it to you."

Black heard a man groaning in the background.

"How's that for proof—"

Black ended the call. Chasity scampered into the kitchen with Bridget behind her.

"What happened? Is my father okay?" she asked, in a shaky voice through quivering lips.

"They called a little early," he said. "Go back to the room."

"No."

Black shrugged. He was upset but in control. *Have it your way*, he thought.

The phone buzzed again, and he answered.

"Who do you think you are? I will kill this—" Ortega started before Black disconnected the call again.

"What are you doing?" Chasity screamed.

Black gave her a hard stare. She looked into his eyes and froze in silence, wide eyes and mouth gaped open. It was as if she was seeing a different person, a side of him she didn't know existed.

Bridget walked over and wrapped her arms around her. "Let's go back in the room," she whispered to her.

Chasity continued to look at him until Bridget spun her in the hall's direction. Black watched them until they cut the corner and vanished out of his line of sight.

The phone hummed again, and Black quickly answered. "I'm not paying for damaged merchandise," he blasted on the line before Ortega could get a word in. "If you want to kill him, go ahead—I'll sleep like a baby tonight either way, but not only will you not see your money—when I wake up tomorrow, I'll make it my mission to hunt you down and bury you. And not for the sake of justice or vengeance, but because I have nothing but time on my hands, and I want to. You asked me who do I think I am? I'm a ghost, a shadow, an enigma. You'll never see me coming until it's too late. There'll be no place—no corner of this world where you can hide that I won't find you. So, this is what's going to happen. You're going to give me a number where I can reach you—we'll pack the money, and when we feel good and ready, we'll call with a time and place for the exchange."

Silence on the line. After a moment, a grunt came through.

"You may want to write this down," Ortega said, faltering with every word.

"Just give it to me."

After Ortega provided the phone number, Black disconnected. He tore a piece of paper from a pad on the kitchen counter and wrote the number down before strolling toward the hallway. It was quiet in the hall, not the faintest noise coming from the room. He knocked on the door and waited as shuffling from the other side drew closer.

Bridget opened the door halfway. "Yeah," she said, slightly rolling her neck.

Black didn't respond, just peered over her shoulder at Chasity sitting on the bed snugging a blanket, and gazing at the floor.

"Excuse me," he told Bridget, pushing the door open and brushing past her.

Chasity looked up as he approached and jabbed the torn piece of paper at her.

"What's this?" she asked.

"It's the number to reach them when you get the cash together."

She grabbed the paper. "What about my father?"

"He's okay. I told them we have the money, and we know they need it. They won't hurt him and risk missing a big payday."

"You told them we have the money? But we don't."

"You do. It's just not in your hands yet. I wanted to keep the carrot dangled in their face. But call Sandra and let her know we bought ourselves some more time and have their number to call and set up the exchange."

"Okay," she said in a low, soft tone, almost apologetic.

"I know you may not approve of my methods—you may not even understand them. But people like this are callous. They only respond when someone is more callous."

Her gaze fell back to the floor.

"I'll be leaving first thing tomorrow morning. Sandra's smart, so I'm confident everything will work out for you."

Black turned to leave the room, and as he did, he saw Chasity glance at him.

"Excuse me," he said again to Bridget on his way out of the room.

THE NEXT HOUR consisted of Black using the bathroom, walking around the front yard, hanging out on the back patio, and finally resting on the couch. He was sitting, unstrapping his dual, knife ankle holsters, when Chasity entered the living room, holding a pillow and blanket. Her hair was down, and she wore plaid black and purple pants with a white tank top.

"Here you go," she said, laying the pillow and blanket next to him.

He dropped his holsters on the floor and slid them under the couch. "Thanks," he said.

She looked at him and smiled. "I should be the one thanking you. I talked with Sandra, told her everything, and she said she'd look into a safe place to have the exchange and make the phone call once we get the money packed up tomorrow."

"That's good news, right?"

She closed her eyes and softly nodded. "You've helped me

so much," she said before opening her eyes. "I couldn't have made it through this day without you."

"Don't mention it."

She chortled at his response and brushed her hair behind her ears before pushing the pillow and blanket aside to sit close to him. "This is going to sound weird," she said, leaning toward him. "I know I just met you today, but it feels like I've known you for a long time."

"I get that a lot."

"You're just that kind of guy, I guess," she said, moving closer to him.

A sweet powdery scent whiffed from her neck and face.

"And what kind of guy is that?" he asked, feeling the warm air breeze from her lips as she moved even closer.

"The kind of guy… a girl wants to kiss."

"Where's Bridget?" he asked when she was within kissing distance.

"Don't worry about her. She's getting ready for bed."

He gently pulled away from her. "Maybe we shouldn't," he said.

She turned her face briefly before looking at him again. "What? I'm not your type?"

"It's not that. I just want you focused."

She scoffed. "Right," she said, staring at him with a crooked smile and reclining on the couch.

"I'm going to get something to drink. You want anything?" he asked, pointing his thumb at the kitchen.

She shook her head.

Black stood and strolled into the kitchen, where he snagged a bottled water from the refrigerator. On his way back to the living room, he heard a dull voice coming from the patio outside in the back. He sat the water on the kitchen island and cracked the door open. Bridget was on the deck in her pajamas, whispering into her phone, her back to him. He opened the door wider, stepped out under the LED lighting and the stars, and walked toward her.

She glanced over her shoulder at him. "Have to call you back," she whispered into the phone before poking the screen and dropping it to her side.

When Black was within two feet of her, she pivoted to face him.

"Hey," she said, forcing a smile.

"Who were you talking to?"

She looked at the screen of her phone and shrugged. "No one."

"You were talking to someone."

"No, I wasn't."

"I just saw and heard you talking to someone."

"That doesn't mean it was someone important," she said, raising her voice. "And why are you worried about who I'm talking to?"

"Why so defensive?"

"Because it feels like you're accusing me of something," she yelled.

He said nothing, just fixed on her and shook his head.

"What?"

Chasity walked outside. "What's going on?" she asked.

Black kept his eyes on Bridget. "I heard your friend here whispering on the phone and wanted to make sure she wasn't talking to someone who knows where we are. But when I asked, she became very defensive," he explained.

"Okay. Who was she talking to?"

"I don't know—why don't you ask her?"

Chasity walked closer to her friend. "So, who were you talking to, Bridget?" she inquired in an unassuming tone.

"No one," Bridget denied.

"Why do you have your phone in your hand?" Black pressed.

She slowly blinked and scoffed.

"Bridget, who were you talking to?" Chasity asked again.

Bridget closed her eyes and pursed her lips, softly shaking her head.

"Bridget," Chasity breathed, snatching the phone from her hand and thumbing through it.

"Look, Chasity, I…"

After five seconds, Chasity's gaze jumped from the phone to Bridget's face. "How long has this been going on?" she asked.

Bridget was silent for a moment, still shaking her head, eyes watering.

Chasity pointed the phone in her face. "How long!" she demanded.

"Chas, it's not like th—"

Chasity dropped the phone and leapt toward her friend, grabbing her hair and yanking her head toward the deck floor.

Bridget bent forward, screaming, flapping her arms over her head, and slapping against the grip of her attacker.

Black grabbed Chasity's wrist, breaking her grip on Bridget before pulling her away, boxing and kicking in his arms.

"You floozy, little tramp!" she yelled.

Bridget flung her hair from her face and adjusted her glasses. "I'm so sorry… I didn't—"

"Liar!" Chasity barked, squirming and pushing Black's arm.

Bridget palmed her hands together. "Chasity, I'm sorry," she apologized, raising her hands to her chin.

The tension paused for a moment, and Black felt the fight in Chasity relax, but it came right back. She jumped in his arms, almost breaking free.

"You better go in the house," Black warned Bridget.

"O-okay," she wept as she zipped inside the door adjoined to the bedroom.

"It's alright, calm down," Black said to a panting Chasity.

"I'm okay—let me go."

Black released her and watched as she put her hands on her hips and circled the patio.

"I can't believe her," she said before fixing on his face.

He said nothing.

"I can't trust anyone," she finished, storming back inside through the kitchen door and slamming it closed behind herself.

Black picked up Bridget's phone from the patio floor and on the screen saw a contact named *Hunk* with a phone number beneath the name. The call history showed about seven calls made to that number throughout the day. He went to the text messages and saw conversations between that same contact filled with: *I love yous, I can't wait to see yous, I miss yous,* but there was one message sent over an hour earlier that stood out. *We're at Paradise Springs Cabin Resort, Cabin 12,* it read.

"Great," he uttered to himself before settling the phone in his pocket and going back inside the house.

Chasity sat on the couch, arms folded, staring straight ahead.

"You okay?" he asked.

She didn't answer. It was a few seconds before she spoke. "I need to get out of here," she said, still gazing out into space.

"Yes, you do."

She looked at him. "What do you mean?"

"Bridget told him where we are."

"So, that's only one other person who knows."

"That's one too many."

"Wait," she said, squinting. "Did you know about this?"

"Yeah."

"How?"

"Rock music."

Chasity said nothing, just looked at him with a blank stare.

"Earlier, at your house when Bridget called, I heard rock music playing in the background. Then at dinner, you told me she's not into rock music, but your ex was, so I figured she'd been with him. It explains her whereabouts during the times you couldn't reach her earlier today."

"Why didn't you tell me?"

"I'd only just figured it out. Plus, it was your ex, and I didn't think it was any of my business."

"Everyone loves to keep things from me."

"Chasity, we don't have time. We need to get you somewhere undisclosed."

She exhaled. "Okay, but only you and me."

Black stood quiet a beat. "Okay," he said. "But we have to leave now."

"Sounds good to me. I'll get my things."

As Chasity rose from her seat, the distant sound of gravel grinding under pressure struck Black's ear. He raised a finger, gesturing for her to remain quiet.

"What?" she whispered.

Black didn't answer, just listened as the sound inched closer. He dashed to the window next to the front door, peeked through the blinds, and saw a pair of headlights glaring up the road. The dark-colored coupe parked next to Bridget's BMW, then the headlights died. The door swung open, and a figure stepped out from behind the wheel.

"Hey. What's out there?" Chasity asked, maintaining a whisper.

Black didn't answer but continued to watch as the figure meandered into the light, slowly revealing their identity.

He turned to Chasity, who was looking at him with wrinkled eyebrows and biting her lip.

"Did you ever call your mother?" he asked.

"I told you I didn't."

"Well, word travels fast," he said, walking to the front door and opening it.

On the other side, standing under the glow of the outside light, was Alice Ball. She jerked her head back and gasped with bulging eyes.

"Oh, the bodyguard. You startled me," she said as she scooted past him into the house.

Black looked her up and down as she entered. She wore the same clothes as earlier, except she now had on flats instead of high heels.

"Mother, what are you doing here?" Chasity asked.

Black shut the door, and Alice jumped at the sound of it closing, glancing over her shoulder at him.

"Spooked?" he said.

Her gaze fell to the floor briefly, and she cut her eyes at him before turning back to Chasity.

"I've been calling, and you haven't been answering," she said.

"That's because I don't want to talk to you—and how did you even find me?"

"Look, sweetheart, I want yo—"

"No, you look! I'm okay, and we—"

"You were right."

"Excuse me?"

"You should call the cops."

Chasity was silent for a beat. "What are you up to?" she said.

Alice sucked in her lips and looked down, softly shaking her head.

Bridget scurried from the hall and stood, watching from across the living room. "Mrs. Alice," she said.

"What did you do?" Chasity continued.

Alice looked up with hollowed cheeks and stared at her daughter.

"Mom?" Chasity whimpered.

"She hired them," Black said. "You hired the kidnappers, am I right?" he went on, fixing on Alice.

She closed her eyes briefly but said nothing.

Chasity kept an unfocused gaze on her.

Black noticed and continued. "Yeah, you hired them, but grabbing your daughter and throwing her in the back of a car wasn't part of your plan. So, I'm guessing that call you were on when we arrived at your house was them, and when they told you what they'd done—you weren't too happy about it. I saw the look on your face when Chasity told you we were held at gunpoint—you were surprised, which leads me to believe they neglected to tell you that part. Now, I'm pretty sure you did this for money, but after Chasity and I left your house, you reconsidered, especially after realizing what you put your daughter through. Maybe you called the kidnappers back after we left and told them it was off, but they made it clear it was happening with or without you."

Alice's breathing became heavy.

Chasity continued to stare at her.

"That's why you made all those calls to Chasity's phone," Black went on. "Because you lost control of the situation and weren't sure how everything would play out. Then there's the question of how you even crossed paths with former cartel members. This one threw me, but then I remembered what you said at your house, about you knowing cops and cops being untrustworthy. Kidman put you in touch with the Larez and Ortega, right? Make sense. Cops are around a lot of criminals. It's the nature of their job."

"But why?" Bridget blurted, but she was looking at Black when she did.

He nodded toward Alice. "I don't know. Why don't you ask her yourself?" he told Bridget.

"No, no, no, no," Chasity started. "My mother is annoying and even heartless at times, but she wouldn't have her daughter's father kidnapped for money, would she?" she shouted, directing the question at her mother.

"I…I needed the money," Alice said with a cracked voice.

Chasity gasped and palmed the sides of her head.

Bridget walked over and placed an arm around her friend.

"Ryan doesn't have a lot of money," Alice continued. "He can't provide the lifestyle I'm accustomed to. And you fired me, so what am I—"

"That's on you, not her," Bridget snapped.

Chasity shrugged Bridget off. "I have to get out of here," she said.

Yeah, me too, Black thought, noticing a shadow through the blinds. He peeped through the window and saw a vehicle creeping up the road, without headlights.

"Were you followed?" he asked Alice.

"I don't believe I was."

Black raced to the couch, picked up his holsters, and strapped them around his ankles.

"Is someone out there?" Bridget asked, walking toward the window.

"Yep, it's them. They're here," he said, making his way back to the window.

"How did they find us?"

"I believe we have *you* to thank for that."

"How's it my fault?"

"You told Calvin where we were. He told her," Black said, nodding at Alice. "And they followed her here," he concluded, guiding Bridget away from the window and peeking through the blinds.

Chasity ducked under him to get a look.

Outside, the dark blue Crown Vic stopped behind and to the side of Alice's car.

"What are we going to do?" Chasity asked, directing the question at Black.

He stepped back from the window and flipped off the

inside light switches near the door. Darkness raced across the foyer, kitchen, and living room areas.

"You three are going to your room. Cut off the light and lock the door," he said.

"No. I'm safer with you," Chasity said.

"Not with what I have planned."

"What is your plan?" Alice asked.

"For the three of you to go to the room," Black ordered.

Bridget began making her way to the room with Alice stumbling behind her, but Chasity stayed.

The clunk of a car door echoed against the side of the cabin.

Black took another look outside and saw three figures exiting the sedan. Two from the front and one from the back. Based on their shape and mannerisms, he quickly identified who each figure was.

"I don't know if I can trust those two. I'm staying with you," Chasity said.

"It's not safe—I need you to go with them."

"Black, my mother—"

"I know what your mother did, but I promise you they're harmless."

She stared at him, and he could see she was struggling to decide.

"Okay, okay," she said. "But what are you going to do?"

"Finish this. Now go. And call the cops."

She made her way to the hall, and Black once again looked out the window into the gloom. The three figures were now close enough that the outside light shined on them. The big guy, Ortega, was on the far left, his pistol aimed at the cabin. In the middle was Larez, holding a handgun down by her side. Kidman was on the far right and had his firearm trained on the cabin. They were seven yards away from the front door, then six, five, and at four, they stopped. There was whispering, and Ortega made a gesture to Kidman, who nodded then aimed his gun to the right side of the cabin and minced toward the back.

Black treaded through the dark and into the kitchen, gently opened the back door, and skulked onto the patio. He crept across the deck, tiptoed down the patio steps, and took cover behind the corner wall, where he heard leaves and twigs crunching under the pressure of footsteps. The noise encroached and grew louder with each step before the barrel of a gun appeared in his peripheral. Black quickly clutched the gun with one hand and pushed against his opponent's wrist with his other until he heard a pop. It was Kidman's trigger finger.

Black immediately took control of the gun and threw his free hand to Kidman's mouth to muffle his pained cry. Black applied force to that same hand, banging Kidman's head against the wall before kneeing him in the gut and using his gun to slap him in the face.

Kidman hit the ground back first and looked up.

Black shook his head. "You're supposed to uphold the law, not break it, punk," he said before putting him to sleep with a kick to the face.

He stuffed Kidman's gun into the back of his pants, patted down Kidman's body, and found a small pistol strapped around his ankle. It was a Ruger LCR. Black removed it from the holster and opened the cylinder, allowing the bullets to drop to the ground before tossing the revolver into the darkness. He dragged Kidman and hid him under the patio deck, then removed Bridget's phone from his pocket and tapped at the screen. The display lit in a blue hue and prompted him for a passcode. He pressed the emergency button, and a dial keypad appeared. He entered *nine-one-one*, then hit call. The phone rang twice before a young lady's voice jumped on the line.

"Nine-one-one, what's your emergency?" she asked.

"There's three of them. They have guns, hurry," Black panted.

"Wait, who has a gun? Where are you?"

"Paradise Springs Cabin Resort. There's two men and a woman, they have guns—we're in cabin twelve—hurry," he ended the call, placing Bridget's phone in his pocket.

He eased inside through the kitchen door and immediately knelt behind the island. It was still dark and quiet until it wasn't. The front door swung open, crashing against the wall, and light beamed inside the cabin. Ortega entered first with Larez following him; both had their guns trained in front of them.

Black reached for the pistol he had taken from Kidman but thought about the group of women in the other room and removed a knife from his ankle holster instead. He peeked, watching as Ortega padded into the living room and Larez into the kitchen. Black kept his eyes on her, and as she trekked just beyond the island, he sprung, grabbing her gun with his free hand and twisting her wrist until the gun dropped. He yanked her arm across her body, pulling her in closer to him, back first with his knife to her neck. It was one smooth motion performed so quickly, it was over before her gun thumped to the floor.

Ortega aimed his gun at them.

"Drop it, carefully," Black demanded.

Ortega kept his gun on them for a beat before finally dropping to one knee and placing his gun on the floor.

"Slide it over."

The compliant man pushed the gun with enough force to where it carried across the floor and spun to a stop in front of Black.

Black kicked the gun further into the kitchen, and still holding Larez, stepped closer to the gun she had dropped and did the same.

He nodded his head toward the foyer. "Go," he instructed Ortega.

The bulky man walked into the foyer, stopping near the window.

"Now, turn on the lights," Black said, inching into the foyer with Larez.

Ortega complied, and radiance filled the cabin, chasing away the remaining dimness.

"Lift your shirt and turn around slowly," Black said, continuing his demands.

The man did as he was told, and Black didn't see any weapons in his pants.

"Pull up your pant legs. One leg at a time."

Again, Ortega obeyed, and again, no additional weapons were visible.

"Okay. Where is he?" Black asked, directing the question at Ortega.

"Who?"

Black felt Larez squirm in his arms after he asked the question. He pulled her arm tighter and pushed his knife deeper into her neck.

"The man you kidnapped."

"Oh. He's outside, waiting in the car," Ortega said, a smirk on his face.

"Good, let's go get him."

At that, Bridget's voice flowed from the hall. "Mrs. Ball, wait," she said.

Black looked from the corner of his eye and saw Alice racing toward the living area. Just as she made it into the living room, he felt Larez pulling away from him. Ortega took advantage of the distraction moving in with a jab. Black remained calm, watching as the fist darted for his face. He released Larez and his knife in the process and sidestepped outside the punch.

Ortega quickly followed up with a swinging back fist.

Black ducked, evading the attack, but Larez wasn't fast enough.

Ortega's fist struck the side of her right jaw, knocking her toward the floor. He tried to catch her, but her spinning descent was too rapid as she fell away from his grip. He watched as she sprawled on the floor. He then turned to Black with wide eyes and flared nostrils, gritting his teeth as he charged his target.

Black relaxed, releasing any tension in his body, the whole situation was as natural as breathing to him, and he didn't move a muscle until he felt Ortega's hands grasp his shoulders. Black countered by spearing both his hands into his opponent's throat.

Ortega coughed and grabbed his own throat while Black followed up with a double punch, striking Ortega in the chest and abdomen simultaneously. The bulky man stumbled backward out the front doorway, reaching for anything to help break his fall, but was unsuccessful and landed on the ground.

Black walked outside and circled him, watching and waiting while the big guy rolled to his stomach and crawled to one knee.

Ortega gave him another dirty look and growled as he sprung to his feet and jumped at him with a flying elbow.

Black shuffled backward and raised his arm above his head, absorbing the attack. He slid back a couple of feet and fought to gain his footing. Ortega rushed him with a right cross. Black slipped under the punch and planted his heel behind his attacker's knee. As Ortega knelt to the ground, Black followed up with an elbow to the back of his neck before putting him in a rear chokehold.

Ortega bucked and swung his body right to left, left to right.

Black held firm, falling backward on the ground for leverage and hooking his legs inside of his adversary's legs.

Ortega continued to sway his body from side to side, gasping for air as he flapped his arms over his head in a desperate attempt to break free.

Black applied steady pressure until Ortega stopped fighting and was barely breathing. He rolled the unconscious man off him, patted him down, and found a set of car keys in his pocket. There was no one in the front or back seats of the Crown Vic, and Black didn't expect there to be. He used the key and popped open the trunk to find a restrained, slender black man with dirty clothes and a stench that suggested he hadn't bathed in days.

Black removed the duct tape from the man's mouth. "Mr. Fox?" he said.

The man nodded. "Yes. Wh—who are you?"

"An ally," Black said, removing a knife from his holster and cutting the tape from the man's hands and feet.

The man crawled out of the trunk and struggled to stand when his feet hit the ground.

Black caught him. "Whoa. You've been in there for some time?"

"Yeah, but I'm fine," the man said, taking a couple of steps unaided. "What's happening?"

"It's a long story, but your daughter is in the cabin. She'll explain it to you."

"Chasity. She's in th—"

Before the man could finish his thought, a thunderous blast roared from the cabin, and then another. They raced to the doorway. Black entered first and saw Larez sitting on the floor with her back against the kitchen island facing the living room. She had her hand pressed to her side. Chasity was in the living room and had a gun aimed at Larez. The gun was shaking along with her hands. A few feet to the right of Chasity, Bridget knelt over Alice, panting and pressing near her shoulder. Blood stained her hands.

Black walked to Larez and picked up the gun that rested a

yard away from where she sat. He ejected the magazine, tossed it into the trash, and cleared the bullet in the chamber before resting the gun on the kitchen countertop.

The man from the trunk entered. He stood at the doorway in a trance.

Black noticed and pointed to Bridget and Alice. "Go help them," he said.

The man rushed and knelt next to his ex-wife. "Alice," he gasped. "Oh, no."

"N—Noah, is that you?" she replied.

Black removed two towels from the counter's drawer and dashed to where Alice lay. "Here, put this on her shoulder and apply pressure," he said, handing Noah a towel. He then walked to Chasity, who still had the gun trained on Larez. "It's okay," he said, touching and lowering the gun.

She dropped the gun to her side and sobbed, burying her face in his chest.

"It's over," Black said.

After a few moments, she gently pulled away from him and looked at her father. "Dad," she said, running to the group.

Black went to Larez. Her face was turning pale, and her eyes looked tired. He knelt and examined the woman, inspecting the wound without touching her.

"Doesn't look like it hit any vital organs," he said, standing and tossing her the second towel. "But if I were you, I'd keep pressure on it until the medics get here," he said, pivoting and walking to Chasity and the others.

They sat Alice upright against the wall and circled her. Bridget was on one knee, pressing the towel against Alice's shoulder while Chasity and Noah craned over the wounded woman.

"How's she doing?" Black asked.

"She was hit in the shoulder but should be fine," Noah answered.

"Mr. Fox," Black said.

"Please, just call me Noah."

"Okay, Noah," Black said, removing the gun he had taken from Kidman and handing it to him. "The other guy is in the back. Just keep an eye on them until the cops come."

"Oh, I never called the cops," Chasity blurted.

"I know you didn't, but I did," he said, pulling a phone from his pocket and giving it to her. "Make sure Bridget gets this," he concluded, walking toward the front door, picking up the knife he dropped earlier and holstering it before continuing outside.

"Hey, wait," Chasity said.

He ignored her, kept walking, and made it three yards from the cabin before he heard her voice again.

"Black," she called.

He turned and waited as she jogged to him.

"Hey, where are you going?" she asked.

"I don't know, south or maybe east."

"No, I mean, why are you leaving?"

Black didn't answer.

"There's still a lot going on. What if I need you?" she continued.

"The rest I can't help you with. You're going to have to work it out with your folks in there."

Chasity sighed.

"And you don't need me. Call Sandra before the cops get here and tell her everything—she'll be able to coach you. And let her know I'd really appreciate it if I'm not investigated for any of this."

"I get the feeling you do this all the time," she said, her voice cracking. "But I'm not good with goodbyes."

Black said nothing.

She threw her arms around his chest and hugged him hard. He hugged her back.

"Sure you don't want to stay?" she said, unwinding from their embrace.

Black nodded. "Take care of yourself," he said.

"You too, Orlando Black," she replied with a sad smile before walking into the cabin.

He watched until she made a left inside and disappeared from his sight. A somber feeling came over him, but as he turned away and looked up at the star freckled sky, he felt at ease.

He made it around the lake before he heard sirens wailing and shortly after flashing red and blue lights coming up the road. Three squad cars raced past him as he briefly stood off to the side and watched. After another five minutes of jogging, he was inside his car. Thirty minutes after that, he was driving on I-15 N, and after another thirty minutes, he was on I-40 E. He saw a sign for a Best Western and exited into a small desert town called Barstow. He parked his car and walked inside. Immediately he heard a TV program running and smelled a diffused, cherry scent wafting in the air. There was no one standing at the counter, but he heard the voice of a news reporter coming from a room behind the desk. He leaned over the counter and saw a messy-haired, middle-aged man in the room with his eyes glued to a flat-screen. Black cleared his throat, and the man jumped.

"I'm sorry," he said, scuttling to the counter. "How can I help you, sir?"

"I'd like a room for the night."

"Alright, let me see what we have," the man said, staring at a computer screen behind the counter while moving and clicking his mouse. "Would you like a double or single bed?"

"Either will do."

"Okay. I got you a single king-size for eighty-five dollars."

Black reached into his pocket and produced a small wad of cash. He handed the receptionist eighty-five dollars exactly.

"Thank you," the man said, sliding a keycard across the countertop. "You can use the elevator down the lobby to your left. And I'm sorry about earlier. I was wrapped up in a story the news was covering. Some multimillionaire's wife divorced him and got a big settlement, and now his son is suing him."

Black grabbed the keycard and pivoted toward the elevators.

"I guess money can't buy a happy home," the man continued.

"No, I guess not," Black replied.

MORE ORLANDO BLACK

YOUR NEXT EXCITING READ IS A PAGE TURN AWAY!

If you enjoyed Family Famous, read on for a preview of Bet On Black, an action-packed, thrilling Orlando Black novel by Alex Cage.

BET ON BLACK

BOOK PREVIEW

CHAPTER
ONE

THERE I STOOD, in the corner of a square ring, under the night sky, in the middle of a valley, and in the middle of another fine mess. A crowd of nearly a hundred surrounded the ring. All yelling and cheering. In the opposite corner stood a muscular man wearing a mohawk and red shorts. Wearing MMA gloves, he pounded his hairy chest before gritting his teeth and narrowing his sights on me. Another man, wearing dark pants and a white shirt, stood at the center of the ring.

The man in the white shirt pointed at me. "Ready, black?" he said. Not because of my name or my skin complexion, but because I wore black trousers and a black tank top.

I nodded.

He then pointed to the guy in the shorts. "Ready, red?"

The hairy-chested man nodded.

"Fight!" the guy at the center of the ring shouted before stepping back.

A bell dinged, and I walked toward the ring's center while the guy in the red shorts raced toward me with his fist drawn back. He swung at my jaw. I bobbed under the punch, then quickly pivoted to face his back with my hands at guard. My opponent spun toward me while hurling a back fist at my head. I ducked beneath the attack and shuffled backward. The crowd's cheers grew louder.

The man's nostrils flared and his teeth gritted as he charged. He threw a kick, but I parried it. As I back-stepped, my attacker shuffled toward me and continued his assault with the combination I was waiting on. He jabbed at me with his left. I parried it. Then his right. I slipped inside the punch, and just as I expected, the man hesitated. In that split second of hesitation, I raised my left arm and exposed my ribcage. My opponent took the bait and launched a kick. Before he could connect, I darted to him and delivered a hard elbow to the side of his face. The man stumbled back and doubled over. I closed the gap between us and kneed his face. As he groaned and flopped backward, I skipped-step toward him and planted my heel into his solar plexus. He landed on the ropes, then flipped over and out of the ring. I followed the referee to the ring's edge and saw my opponent sprawled on the floor.

The referee ducked between the ropes, then knelt and lifted the man's head from the ground before saying something to him and moving the fingers of his free hand in the fighter's face. After a few seconds, the ref stood, crossed his arms, then slung them apart. The bell dinged, and the referee crawled back into the ring and raised my arm. Cheers and applause came from the crowd as I snatched my arm away from the ref and turned toward my corner. The person I was looking for wasn't there, so I scanned the other three corners, but still couldn't find him.

As I hopped from the ring, two men hoisted the guy in the red shorts to his feet. I walked past and threaded through the crowd with my head on a swivel, searching for the missing DEA agent. The pats on my back and shouts from the crowd followed me all the way to a passageway for the locker room. I walked through the passage alone and to a dirt field illuminated by large construction flood lights. A pair of mobile homes flanked me on either side. A third home sat on the far end with a flagpole out front. That was where the lockers were. As I made my way across the field toward it, a guard armed with an MP5 approached me.

"Good fight, Ghost," he said with a smile. "You're so quick, the fight didn't even last that long. I bet on you, so I made some money tonight."

"That's great," I said. "The guy I was with earlier, have you seen 'em?"

The guard pursed his lips and shook his head. "Not since he was with you."

"Alright. Thanks," I said before continuing toward the portable home.

"See you around, champ," the guard said to my back.

The portable home was empty inside. I hustled to the locker room, opened my locker, then changed into my jeans and t-shirt. Before slipping into my boots, I made sure my dual knife holsters were secure around my ankles. Once fully dressed, I checked my phone, but found no missed calls or messages. I exited the portable and walked back to the ring area, where the crowd roared in encouragement for an ongoing match. Weaving through the mob, I kept an eye out for my missing DEA agent, but there was still no sign of him. I continued through the crowd, then into a passageway which led out of the valley.

As I exited the passageway, two men in black suits armed with MP5s stood on either side of the entrance. One of them nodded at me as I dodged a line of people and walked onto an enormous field full of parked cars. And not just any cars. Bentleys, Ferraris, and Lamborghinis were all present, but the car I was looking for wasn't as extravagant. It was a dented, silver Ford Focus in need of new tires and a new paint job. When I located the car, I peeked through the window hoping to find the DEA agent who also happened to be my chauffeur but was disappointed when he wasn't there and wondered how I'd get back to my motel room since he had the car's key.

At that thought, I heard a fuss coming from the passageway entrance. When I glanced over my shoulder, I saw the missing agent exiting, but he wasn't alone. Two men trailed behind him. Both were fit, both had ivory skin, both wore a suit with no tie, but one had spiky blond hair while the other had short brown hair. A short man with a gray suit and a ponytail followed close behind them, carrying a brief-case. While keeping my eyes on the group of men, I ducked and circled the Ford's trunk to the passenger side. They all entered a black Porsche Cayenne before cruising out of the parking area and up the dirt road. I removed a knife from my ankle holster, then raced to the front driver's side door of the Focus. With my face turned from the door, I smashed the butt of the knife into the window. The glass shattered, and I used my knife to rake away the loose shards before reaching my arm through and unlocking the door. Using the knife, I poked the steering column and pried it open, then spend the next few minutes relearning how to hot wire a car. When I connected the correct wires, the Focus revved to life. I swept the glass from the seat and slid in behind the wheel. I backed from the parking area, flicked on the headlights, then sped down the road. The road was dim and the Cayenne was nowhere in sight. Not a glint from a taillight, not even a silhouette of the vehicle, just darkness.

Lost them. Not good.

After a minute of driving, I approached two SUVs parked perpendicular on either side of the road. Neither one was the Cayenne. At each SUV, there was the shadow of a man holding a gun. I slowed down and one of them recognized me and nodded. After returning the nod, I rode past. I monitored them in my rear-view mirror until they completely disap-peared into the darkness of the night. The Focus droned up the rough, dirt road for another twenty minutes before smooth pavement caressed its tires. I removed my phone, flipped it open, pressed at it, and held it to my ear. It rang and rang, but no one answered.

"Another missing agent," I muttered to myself. "Not good."

I drove another hour before trying the number again. And like before, no answer.

Where are you?

After stopping for gas and driving another forty minutes, I arrived at my motel, but I didn't pull into the parking lot because something caught my attention. The Porsche Cayenne sat parked a few spaces from my room. I made a note of the license plate number, then continued a quarter of a mile up the road before turning into a local diner's parking lot. Inside the diner, the smell of burgers and fries and customer chit chat filled the space, and as I made my way to the counter eyes from unknown faces followed me. I grabbed a napkin and a to-go menu off the countertop before hearing a voice.

"Hi," the voice said.

I turned to see a slim woman with silky dirty-blonde hair approaching me.

She smiled. "Gonna have dinner with us, Mr. White?"

It took me a split second to process everything before saying, "I sure am, but I'm going to take it to go."

"Ahh, you're not staying here with me tonight?"

"Nope. I'm sorry," I said with a smile.

She smiled again. "So, what are you having?"

"I'll have what I had last night."

"Grilled chicken, brown rice, and steamed broccoli, right?"

"You remembered," I said with my eyebrows raised.

"Of course. Most people around here don't eat like that. I'll get this in for you," she said as she pivoted away from me.

"Thanks—hey."

The waitress turned to face me.

"Do you have a pen?" I asked.

"Sure. Plenty of 'em," she said while handing me a pen from her apron pocket.

"Thanks."

She smiled, then made her way toward the kitchen.

On the napkin I wrote, *After the fight, Vargas left with Long, Snyder, and a short man with a ponytail. Black Porsche Cayenne LPN MXC-F144*, then finished with, *It's parked in front of my motel room*. At the top, I wrote the date and time, then used the menu to create an envelope before placing the napkin inside and folding it shut. I exited the diner, crossed the street, and walked twenty yards in the motel's direction before reaching a slightly worn mail drop box. I placed the folded menu inside, then made my way back to the diner where I sat at the counter for five minutes before the waitress brought me my food.

"Here you go," she said while placing my bag and ticket on the table.

The bill was eighteen dollars. I gave her thirty.

"That's all yours," I said.

"Thanks. Will I see you for dinner tomorrow?"

"Possibly. And maybe the next few days after."

"Well, I'll be here tomorrow night, but the next few nights after, I'll be working late at the mall. There's a large shipment coming in, and we're rearranging the store. Just in case you come and I'm not here."

"I'll keep that in mind," I said on my way to the door.

"See you around, Anthony."

I entered the Focus and placed my food on the passenger seat and removed my flip phone. I tried the number I called earlier and again got no answer.

Something's off.

I backed the car out and veered onto the road toward the motel. The Cayenne was no longer there. I parked, grabbed my food, then walked to my motel room. Before opening the door, I placed my ear to it and listened, but heard nothing. Multiple scenarios played in my mind. They could've really left, or were lurking around waiting to ambush me, but for what? I was sure they didn't want to physically harm me, so I unlocked my door and opened it. And when I saw inside, suddenly I wasn't so sure anymore.

CHAPTER
TWO

TRUTH BE TOLD, I wasn't completely sure about anything since two days prior, when it all started. I was driving through a small town five miles west of San Antonio, Texas. It was a sunny and comfortable afternoon, and I had just finished gassing up my black Dodge Viper GTS when I heard a faint grunt. I walked to the opposite side of the empty gas station and saw a group of men tussling in the dirt near the back of the station. My gut told me to go back to my car and leave, because given my history, my good deeds usually cost me a day or even a week of headache. Going against my better judgment, I walked across the pavement and onto the dry grainy dirt where three men stood in front of me. Two on one side, and one on the other, all with their fists raised. The two standing together looked similar. Both wore jeans and a t-shirt. Both had toned physiques and ivory freckled skin, but one had spiky blond hair while the other had short brown hair. The guy opposite them wore dark blue jeans and a dirty white polo shirt. His hair was dark and messy, and his beard and mustache were bushy on his almond-colored face. The man with the short brown hair feinted a jab at the man across from him. Keeping his fist raised, the guy in the polo shirt shuffled back with his eyes locked on the two men in front of him.

"Now two on one, that doesn't seem fair," I said to the group of men.

The guy with the blond hair glanced over his shoulder. "Mind your business and move along," he said.

At that moment, the brown-haired guy threw a cross and connected to the jaw of the man with the bushy beard. The man fell to the ground and a cloud of dust rose around him. He rolled to his side and crawled to a kneeling position.

"No, I think I'll stick around and see how this plays out," I said before walking toward the fallen man. Halfway there, I heard footsteps closing in behind me.

"I thought I said get lost," the blond guy's voice growled.

As I turned, his fist darted toward my face. I weaved outside of his punch and delivered a solid hook to the guy's ribcage. He dropped to the ground and wormed in the dirt as his partner with the low cut directed his attention at me.

"You'll pay for that," he said, knitting his eyebrows and gritting his teeth.

I shrugged and rolled my eyes.

The man pivoted on his right leg before kicking at me with a roundhouse. I stepped inside his attack, caught his kicking leg at my side, and hooked it with my arm before sweeping his other leg from under him. It happened in one quick, smooth motion. So quick, the guy didn't realize it happened until he descended to the ground. I saw the whites of his eyes grow larger and his mouth open wide as he plummeted. When his back smacked the ground, I heard a breath forced from his mouth. I shook my head at the sight of the two men squirming on the ground, then walked to the bushy bearded guy.

"How did you get on their bad side?" I asked, while grabbing his arm and helping him to his feet.

And to my surprise, the guy yanked his arm away, then shoved me.

"Whatcha do?" he said.

"Thought I was helping you."

"I never asked for help, amigo."

"So, you enjoy getting punched in the face?"

The man's gaze fell to the ground, then on the two men in the dirt, then back to me before finally across the highway, beyond a parked dark-blue sedan, and into the desert field.

After a few seconds, and no verbal response from him, I shrugged and walked back to my car. I got behind the wheel and watched as the bushy faced guy helped the other two men to their feet. The three walked further behind the gas station. The bushy bearded guy kept peering over his shoulder and across the highway at the dark-blue sedan.

When the men were out of sight, the sedan slowly pulled off. I found it strange, but an hour earlier I saw a woman casually walking around the outside of a Whataburger with an assault rifle, and no one batted an eye. And thirty minutes before that, I saw a man eat a cinnamon roll the size of his head, so three guys fist fighting wasn't too shocking or unbelievable. I started my car, veered onto the highway, and drove eight miles southeast until I reached a hotel. Figured I'd turn in for the day and continue heading east the next day. I checked in at the front desk, then went to my room, carrying only a change of jeans and a white t-shirt with me. A pine smell struck my nose as I entered. Light permeated through a large window and filled the spacious room. I tossed my clothes on the bed before patting the comforter. The linen was soft and wrinkle free, perfect for a good night's sleep. And I wouldn't find out until the next day just how much I'd need it.

• • •

I rolled from the bed and onto the floor early the next morning. Inside the dim room, I performed two hundred push-ups, then one hundred sit-ups followed my thirty minutes of forms and shadow boxing before concluding with some tai chi movements and breathing exercises. The sun had risen above the horizon by the time I'd finished a steamy shower and shrugged into my clothes. I brushed the bushy hair on my head and face before concluding I should see a barber soon. My stomach growled and since I skipped dinner the night before, the next thing on my mind was breakfast.

Downstairs, the aroma from eggs, grits, sausage, biscuits, and coffee stuffed the area. It was the smell of the typical continental breakfast. I thanked the dining room staff and ate a bit of everything before washing it down with black coffee and heading to the front desk.

"Checking out," I said to a slender, dirty-blonde woman behind the desk while handing her my keycard.

"Thank you, sir. How was your stay?" she asked as she typed on a keyboard.

"Brief."

She smiled and typed for a few more seconds before looking at me and saying, "Okay, sir, you're all taken care of."

"Thank you," I told her before walking out of the hotel.

I went to my car and placed my dirty clothes in the trunk, and as I circled to the front of the Viper, I heard a voice.

"Hot ride," a woman said.

I glanced in the voice's direction and saw a woman approaching. She wore boots, jeans, and a brown biker jacket. Her skin was a silky espresso tone, slightly darker than mine, and her eyes hid behind a pair of shades.

"Thanks, she's a beauty," I said, while scanning the parking lot.

"That she is," the woman said. She then used her fingers to rake strands of her natural, shoulder-length, curly hair behind her ear.

As she walked to the Viper's hood and leaned against it, I caught a glimpse of her badge and gun. I glanced around the parking lot and spotted the same dark-blue sedan I saw the day before. It sat parked at the front of the hotel, near the east far corner.

I nodded in the sedan's direction. "You have a hot ride, too."

She followed my gaze, then placed her sights back on me before scoffing and smiling. "Yeah, I guess so," she said with a chuckle, still leaning on the hood.

"Well, we both have hot rides. I'll be on my way now."

"Not so fast, Mr. Orlando James Black," she said standing from the car.

"Oh, you used my full name. I must be in trouble."

"Maybe. That all depends on you," she said while waving the sedan over.

As the vehicle pulled from the parking space, she placed her hand near her hip, on the same side as her firearm.

"What are you carrying, Glock 19?"

"No, a seventeen, and I'm pretty good with it."

I chuckled. "I bet you are. Mind telling me what you're doing?"

"I will."

The sedan stopped beside us, and from the front passenger's side, a woman with caramel hair flowing down her back exited. She had tanned skin, and her height and clothing matched the other woman's except her biker jacket was black instead of brown.

"Aren't you required to tell me who you are?" I asked the woman with the natural, curly hair.

"Am I?"

"Yeah, usually law enforcement is. Dark sedan, Glock 17. I'm guessing you're not local law enforcement. What are you DEA, FBI?"

"Special Agent Deidra Harris, DEA," she said while flapping her jacket and exposing her badge.

I'd seen fake badges before, but hers wasn't one of them. It was legit.

"Okay, Agent Deidra Harris, what do you want with me?"

"We'll get to that," she said as the woman with the caramel-colored hair approached us. Deidra pointed at her. "This is Special Agent Jessica Ward."

Jessica's eyes slowly traced from my feet to my face. She then leaned toward Deidra. "He's handsome," she said.

Deidra scoffed a chuckle, and as she did, the sedan's front driver's side door opened. On the opposite side of the roof, the upper body of a stocky man with silver hair appeared. He circled the car to where the group of us stood.

"This is Special Agent William Anson," Deidra said introducing him.

Anson rubbed his hand across his silver, full beard and just stared at me.

"Okay, now what?" I asked with a shrug.

"We're going for a ride," Deidra said.

I glanced at my car, then back at her.

"Don't worry, Mr. Black," she said. "Your car will be fine."

"Are you charging me with something?" I asked.

"Not at the moment."

"Then I don't have to take a ride with you—"

"But I can charge you with obstruction," she said interrupting me.

"Obstruction?"

"Yep. So, either come quietly, or in cuffs. The choice is yours."

I stared at her for a moment before sighing and walking toward the sedan's back passenger side door.

"You can ride shotgun," she said while pointing to the front door. "I insist."

I shook my head before walking to the door, opening it, and sliding into the sedan. Deidra and Jessica entered the back while Anson sat behind the wheel.

Another fine mess, I thought, as Anson started the car and pulled out of the parking lot.

CHAPTER
THREE

TEN MINUTES LATER, we veered into the driveway of a gated, eight-story, off-white brick building in downtown San Antonio. Anson lowered his window as he stopped at the guard hut. A security guard stepped out, then waved Anson through as if he knew him. Anson drove inside and toward the parking garage, where he found a spot close to the entrance. We exited the car, entered the building, and walked past a security station in an empty lobby before taking the elevator to the fifth floor. The elevator dinged, the doors slid apart, and we stepped into a foyer where a pair of large glass double doors met us.

"I got it," Jessica said, while lifting a card from her pocket and waving it across a small square panel next to the double doors.

The doors clicked, and Jessica pulled open one side.

"C'mon in, Mr. Black," Deidra said as she walked through the doorway.

I followed her in while Jessica held the door open. Anson grabbed the door and nodded for Jessica to enter before him.

"Such a gentleman," she said.

Anson grunted.

I followed Deidra down a short hallway and onto an office floor. At the center were cubicle desks and computers and tables. Individuals walked up and down the floor and conversed with one another.

"This way, Mr. Black," Deidra said pointing to her right.

The four of us walked in that direction, passing more office furniture and agents on our way to a room. Inside was a rectangular table with two chairs across from one another.

"Have a seat, Mr. Black," Deidra said.

I stared at her for a moment before shaking my head and walking toward the chair facing the door. On my way, I noticed a double-sided mirror to my right.

"I'll be in my office if you girls need anything," Anson said before leaving the room.

"Make yourself comfortable, Mr. Black," Deidra said. "Do you want anything? Water or coffee?"

"I'll take a coffee," I said.

Deidra nodded at Jessica, who walked toward the door before turning and asking me, "How do you take your coffee? Cream and sugar?"

"Straight black, please."

Jessica smiled, then walked out of the room.

"I'll be back," Deidra said as she walked to the door herself.

"How long are you going to keep me here?" I asked.

"Shouldn't be too long, but that'll largely depend on you," she said before exiting the room.

As the door clunked shut, I sat and stared in its direction, drumming my fingers on the tabletop. Three minutes later, Jessica entered the room with a steaming, white Styrofoam cup in hand.

She placed the cup on the table. "Anything else I can get you?"

"Answers," I said.

"Deidra will fill you in," she said before smiling and walking out.

Fill me in? I thought, while sipping my coffee. I drank half the cup before the door opened and Deidra entered, carrying a manilla folder. She dropped the folder on the table as she sat in the chair across from me. I looked into her eyes. They showed strength and vulnerability.

"Okay, Mr. Black. Who are you, really?" she asked.

I shrugged. "You've been calling me Mr. Black all morning, so let's stick with that." I nodded toward the double mirror. "Do we have an audience?"

Deidra's eyebrows knitted. "Audience?" she said while looking at the mirror. "No, this'll be a private conversation. Just between you and I."

"What's in the folder?"

"You."

I squinted.

Deidra picked up the folder and opened it. "Let's see," she said, looking into the folder. "In the foster system at a very young age. Wow, they sure kept you in a lot of different martial art classes growing up." She read in silence for a moment. "Huh. Your senior year of high school was very interesting," she said while looking at me with a raised eyebrow.

I said nothing.

"Okay. So you went into the army, spent some time as a Ranger and a Delta Force member. Very impressive. Then there's a few years of redaction before you settled in Asia." Deidra closed the folder and dropped it on the table. "Who are you?" she asked.

I shrugged and nodded at the folder. "I guess I'm whatever's in there," I said.

Deidra crinkled her nose and shook her head. "Nah, that was then. Who are you now?"

"Are you charging me with something?"

Deidra hunched her shoulders and stood. "I don't want to," she said as she walked to the door.

I watched as she opened it and waved to someone on the outside.

"But I can," she continued, walking back to the table.

Seconds later, a familiar-looking man with a folder in his hand entered the room and stood next to her. *The bushy beard guy from yesterday.* Except today he'd cleaned up and wore a fitted, navy-colored suit. Still had a beard, but he looked much younger than he did yesterday.

"You remember Agent Vargas from yesterday, right?" Deidra said.

Vargas extended his hand to me. "Richard Vargas, sir," he said.

I looked at his hand, then stared at him.

He pulled his hand back.

"What's going on?" I asked, turning my attention to Deidra.

She sighed and sat in the chair. "Mr. Black, you've single-handedly halted months of investigative work."

"I'm working undercover," Vargas said. "Those guys you saw me fighting were my way in."

"Your way into what? The hospital?" I said.

"I could've taken them."

"Not from where I was standing."

"Either way," Deidra said. "You've stalled our investigation, and you're gonna help get us back on track."

"And why would I do that? I was only trying to help an innocent civilian."

"Richard is a government agent. He was working a case that your actions hindered. That's called obstruction."

"You know that won't stick."

Deidra leaned back in the chair and folded her arms. "Maybe, maybe not. But it'd be a lot easier on you if you just cooperate," she said while tapping her biceps with her fingers.

I stared at her for a moment. We locked eyes, and she glanced away briefly before looking at me again and forcing a smile.

Someone's uneasy. "Cooperate how?"

Deidra's eyebrows rose, and she unfolded her arms. "So, you're going to play ball? Good choice."

"Just tell me what's going on."

"Right to business. I like it," she said before looking at Vargas and opening her hand.

Vargas gave her the folder he carried.

Deidra opened the folder, placed it on the table near me, and pointed to a man's head shot. "This is Christopher Navarro," she said.

He had smooth, tan skin, dimples, and combed-back hair. His picture should have been on a modeling agent's desk instead of a table inside of a government agency.

"He's part of the Escarra cartel," Deidra said.

"The cartel, great. Sounds like a fun bunch," I said under my breath.

"What's that?"

"Nothing."

"Okay. Well, as you can imagine, they're into drugs, human, and gun trafficking. All the crimes fitting of a cartel."

I sighed. "Yeah, that's what cartels do."

"This one takes part in somewhat of an… unusual activity. At least as far as cartels go."

I shrugged. "Let me guess, it's underground fighting?"

"Yes, you catch on quickly. Navarro is his cartel's representative for these organized fight groups. We were planting Vargas inside the organization. That is, before you obstructed his efforts."

"So now you want me to infiltrate the organization as a

fighter? And for my troubles, I won't be charged with obstruction."

Deidra's eyes widened and her lips parted. "Sharp. You really do understand."

I shook my head. "No. There's a lot I don't understand." *Like why are you willing to stoop so low just to make this case?* "Why is the DEA investigating underground fights? If you know Navarro is involved with running drugs, bust him on that. I mean… Drug Enforcement Administration, the word drug is in the agency's name."

"It's a process," Deidra said before closing the folder and handing it to Vargas.

"Right."

She stood from the table. "Come with me. I want to show you something."

I stood and followed her and Vargas out of the room.

"I'll catch up with you later," Vargas told Deidra, on our exit.

"Alright," she said before looking at me. "C'mon, this way."

We walked through the center of the office floor and into another room that housed three desks. Two were empty, and Jessica stood at the third with a document in hand. Near the back of the room, a paper-littered table sat flush with the wall. And at the far back wall stood an investigative board.

Deidra walked to the desk across from Jessica's. "Look who decided to play ball," she said to her.

Jessica smiled and looked at me. "Really? Welcome to the madness."

I shrugged but said nothing.

"Give me just a second, Mr. Black. Make yourself comfortable," Deidra said as she sat at her desk. She nodded toward a small room to my left. "If you want more coffee, there's some in the break room."

I walked toward the back of the room. On my way, I

noticed a picture on the third desk. In the picture was Vargas with a woman, a boy, and a girl. *Must be his family*, I thought as I continued to the investigative board.

The board had a few pictures, and marker-drawn lines connected them. There was a picture of Navarro with the words Escarra Cartel written below it. To the right of the picture was a face I'd never seen before with Ramos Cartel written at the bottom. Both pictures had lines drawn to a pair of images above them. In those pictures were the two guys I saw Vargas fighting with earlier. The image with the blond spiky-haired man had the name Ethan Long written next to it, and his partner with the short brown hair had the name Kody Snyder written next to his. Both their pictures had a line connecting them to a question mark drawn inside of a circle at the top of the board.

"Getting familiar with the case, Mr. Black?" Deidra said, approaching me.

"Not sure what I'm looking at, and you can stop calling me Mr.," I said.

"This is what I wanted to show you. Some faces should look familiar," she said as she stepped to the board.

"I recognize a few of them."

"We need to figure out who this is," she said, pointing at the question mark on the board. "This person is the reason the DEA is investigating an underground fighting ring. Whoever he is, he's in charge of the fight club and is supplying multiple cartels with drugs and financing."

"What's your plan for getting me in?" I asked.

"Vargas has some contacts to get you started with some small fights. From there, you'll work your way up to the high-profile fights where the big fish are."

"This sounds like it'll take a while."

Deidra shook her head. "That all depends on how good of a show you put on."

I stared at her.

"According to our intel, there will be a big fight in three days. They're looking for a challenger for the current champion. Lots of money involved, so we're positive whoever's pulling the strings will be there. I'd like to get you in that fight."

"Three days? It's going to take at least a week to prep and train."

Deidra shook her head again. "We don't have a week. We're working on getting your first fight later this afternoon."

"What? Are you tryin' to get me killed?"

"Don't be so dramatic, Black. I've read your file and seen you fight. This will be a cakewalk for you."

"I'm not worried about the fighting, but what about the cartels and this well-connected supplier?"

"Let us worry about that."

I stared at her again, but this time harder.

"Don't worry. We got you covered, you know?" she said before biting her bottom lip.

"We need more time, or this may come back to haunt us."

"We're ready now, and you have no choice."

"What if I don't win my fights?"

Deidra paused for a moment and inhaled before exhaling a shaky breath. "I'm not worried about that, because I know you can handle yourself. But if you happen to lose... well, the obstruction charges will be waiting for you."

"So, I basically get nothing for my efforts?"

"Sorry, Black, but failure is not an option here."

"There's something you're not telling me, but it'll all come out. I have a way of getting to the bottom of things."

Deidra forced a smile. "Well then, it should be easy for you to figure out who's our big question mark. C'mon, I'll explain more on the way to pick up your car."

I followed Deidra toward the front of the office. She stopped at Jessica's desk on the way.

"I believe we now have Mr. Black's full cooperation. I'm taking him to get his car," she told her partner.

Jessica squinted. "Are you sure? You don't want me to come?" she asked.

Deidra looked at me. "No, I'll be fine. I think we have an understanding, right, Black?"

I looked at her and shook my head. "Whatever," I said as I brushed past her and walked toward the door.

It took Deidra and me four minutes to make it downstairs and to the parking garage. Three minutes after that, we were on the road with her behind the wheel and me in the front passenger's seat. I was looking outside of my window at some road construction when I heard Deidra's voice.

"This won't be as bad as you think, Black," she said.

I looked at her and felt my eyebrows furrow as I did.

She glanced at me before looking back at the road. "We'll have your back, and it's not like you can't handle yourself."

"You're not very convincing," I said as I turned to my window and watched the trees and buildings roll by.

Deidra sighed. "We'll keep your car at HQ and set you up in a motel, you know, so you can maintain your cover."

I shrugged. "Whatever."

"Black, I'm gonna need you to get your head in the game."

"You act like you're paying me for this or something."

"Not charging you is payment. You don't have much of a choice."

"If you say so."

Deidra looked at me before shaking her head, then facing the windshield. "You should know these monsters have ruined many people's lives. Innocent people. Some—some really good people. I will not let them get away with it," she said with her eyes focused on the road.

I shrugged and looked out my window for the rest of the short, quiet drive. When we arrived at the hotel's parking lot, Deidra parked the sedan next to my Viper. I slid out of the sedan and circled to my car. As I did, Deidra rolled down her window.

"Stay close behind me," she said.

"Yeah, yeah. I got it," I said as I entered the Viper and started the engine.

Deidra pulled out of the parking lot, and I followed her back to the DEA's headquarters. We veered into the driveway, and she stopped at the security hut and exchanged some words with the guard. A moment later, the guard waved both of us through. We parked in the garage, entered the building together, and rode the elevator up to the fifth floor before walking to her office. Inside, both Jessica and Vargas sat at their desks.

Vargas stood with a sheet of paper in hand. "There you are," he said while walking to Deidra and me. He handed Deidra the paper. "I managed to get him in this fight. It's a small one, but there may be some big players there."

Deidra glanced down at the document and smiled. "Good work," she said.

"And his motel room is all ready," Jessica said as she stood and walked to us.

"Great. Let's iron out the details."

"Please do," I said.

Everyone looked at me.

"I'm the one who's going in. The one whose life is on the line, but I know the least about this plan I never agreed to."

Deidra sighed. "Black, your part is simple. Just put on a great show and gather any information that'll help us identify the question mark," she said, pointing at the investigative board in the back. "We have places where you can meet us or leave a message regarding your progress or any concerns you have."

"Also, there's this," Jessica said, walking back to her desk. She removed a flip phone and charger from her drawer. "This phone is programmed for secure communication. Deidra is your primary contact for this operation, so when you call her, the line will be encrypted. And the phone won't hold any information about the call, but it only does that for her phone number, so you'll have to memorize it." She handed me the phone and charger.

"Alright. That shouldn't be a problem," I said, while placing both the phone and charger in my pocket.

Deidra walked to her desk, grabbed a pen, and wrote on a sticky note before walking back and giving it to me. "This is my number. Like Jessica said, memorize it."

I looked at the number, committed it to memory, and handed the paper back to her. It took all of three seconds.

"Got it?" she asked.

"Really?"

She folded her arms and cocked her head to the side.

I sighed as I removed the flip phone from my pocket and dialed the number. The phone rang twice before Deidra's pocket buzzed.

She removed her phone and tapped at it. "Hello," she said into it.

I heard her through the phone and said, "I got it," before ending the call and jabbing the flip phone back into my pocket.

Deidra rolled her eyes and did the same with her phone. "Okay, you have an excellent memory. Should make things easier since I won't have to repeat myself. The first important detail you need to remember is, for the duration of this operation, you're not Orlando Black. You'll be Anthony White."

"That's original."

"As mentioned, you'll be put up in a motel, and that'll be your home. We'll provide you with money for food, personal care, and any other items you may need for this operation. Contact me anytime if you need something."

Vargas went to his desk and returned with another sheet of paper. "Here's a couple of addresses where you can leave us a message if things get sticky, or the phone stops working or you can't reach us. They're within walking distance of the motel."

I took the paper and memorized the locations before handing it back to him.

"At each spot there's a mailbox—which isn't really a mailbox, but you can drop your message in there. We'll be checking them periodically if we don't hear from you. But this is just in case of an emergency."

"And if you have to use this method of contact," Deidra said, "make sure you're not followed."

I shrugged. "Right."

"Also, anything that can identify you as Orlando Black, you'll have to leave here."

"Speaking of which. What about the two guys you were fighting, Vargas? Long and Snyder? Won't they recognize me?"

Vargas shook his head. "You were so fast. I don't think they remember what you looked like. When we talked after, neither one could describe you in any detail."

I nodded. "That may be true but seeing someone more than once could raise suspicion."

"He's right," Deidra said.

"Okay, what do you have in mind?" Vargas asked.

Deidra's eyes traced from my feet to the top of my head. "Black, how do you normally keep your hair?"

"It's usually a low-fade," I said. "But haven't had a cut or shave in a couple of weeks."

"More like over a month. But don't worry, the agency will take care of it for you, in-house."

"Good idea, but I don't let just anyone cut my hair."

"You mean you want a barber experienced in cutting black men's hair?"

"Suffice it to say, I don't wanna be walking around with a soup bowl."

Deidra laughed.

Jessica's eyebrows knitted. "What's a soup bowl?" she asked.

"I wouldn't do you like that, Black," Deidra said. "Don't worry, this guy has years of experience cutting hair like yours."

Anson entered the room as Deidra was speaking.

"I was just talking about you," she said.

"Are we ready?" Anson asked.

"Almost, but we'll need you to give Black a cut."

I stepped to Deidra's side. "Are you serious?" I whispered in her ear.

"Trust me, he's good," she whispered back.

"Well, c'mon, kid," Anson said while waving me over. "I don't have all day."

As I walked toward the door, I heard Deidra giggling behind me. I turned and looked at her and smiled, then followed Anson out of the office. We walked across the busy office floor, down a hall, then into a ten-by-fifteen room. As I entered, I felt a slight drop in temperature and a citrus aerosol fragrance struck my nose. Inside, a countertop occupied by clippers, trimmers, shavers, and cosmetic products ran the length of the room. Hanging above the countertop were three mirrors equally spaced along the wall. Three swivel chairs sat in front of each mirror, and on the opposite side of the room rested a sink, dryer, and a small table where more cosmetics lay.

"Well, take a seat," Anson said while pointing toward the swivel chairs.

I walked to the chair closest to the back and sat.

Anson met me there before turning me toward the mirror, opening a drawer under the counter, and removing an apron. He flapped the apron and threw it around me.

"So how long have you've been cutting hair?" I asked him.

Anson picked up a set of clippers. "Too long. Almost as long as I've been with the agency," he said, before spraying the blades with some type of aerosol disinfectant.

"How long have you been with the agency?"

"Twenty-nine years. Twenty-five of those years I've cut hair."

"That is a long time."

Anson used a towel to wipe the blades. "How do you want your hair?" he asked.

I looked at him in the mirror. "You know how to do a low-fade?"

"I sure do. My partner wore a low-fade, and I used to cut his hair all the time."

"Used to?"

"Yeah. He was killed on duty two years ago."

"Sorry to hear that."

"It happens."

"Given your seniority, I take it you're in charge of this operation."

Anson sighed. "No. I'm just support. My sight and hearing isn't what it used to be. I wouldn't be much help in the field."

"So, Deidra is running the show?"

Anson sighed again. "Yeah. I've tried to get her to hand it off to someone else, but she's stubborn."

"I noticed."

Anson chuckled. "I bet you have," he said while picking up a comb and sliding it through my hair.

"Why'd you want her to hand it off?"

"Enough talking," Anson said with a grunt. "Be still or you may end up looking like a leopard."

I sat still and quiet with many questions in my head while Anson flipped on the clippers.

• • •

Forty-five minutes later, Anson used the towel to wipe the loose hair from around my neck and flapped the apron from around me. I looked into the mirror and saw someone I hadn't seen in two weeks, or over a month, if I let Deidra tell it. I turned to my right side, then my left.

"You did a really good job. Thanks," I said.

"Like I said, I've been doing it for quite some time," Anson said as he walked to the back corner and grabbed a broom and dustpan.

I stood from the chair and further inspected myself in the mirror, and as I did, the door swung open and Jessica entered.

"They need to see you back in the office," she said to me, slightly out of breath.

CHAPTER
FOUR

"OKAY, WHAT'S GOING on?" I asked.

"I'll explain on the way," Jessica said.

I walked through the door and into the hall.

Jessica smiled as I passed her. "You look even cuter with a haircut," she said before looking back at Anson. "We'll fill you in."

Jessica and I walked back to the office and found Deidra and Vargas standing near Deidra's desk.

"There you are," she said as she examined my haircut. "It looks good."

"Thanks," I said.

She handed me two sheets of paper. "Here, memorize this. It's your new identity. Your fight's been moved up an hour, so we're gonna have to move."

"I'll go change my clothes," Vargas said on his way toward the door.

I looked at the document and saw a picture of me with the name Anthony White next to it. Apparently, I grew up in Connecticut as a troubled youth and went to prison for armed robbery and attempted murder.

"You got it?" Deidra asked me.

I nodded. "Yeah, the gist of it."

"Black, I need you to have it down."

"I will if I can have more than five seconds to review the cover," I said, walking toward the back of the office.

As I continued to review my cover dossier, Deidra and Jessica stood whispering. It appeared Deidra was giving out orders until she tilted her head back on an inhale, then hung it toward the floor on an exhale.

Jessica placed a hand on her colleague's shoulder. "It'll be okay," she said.

Deidra lifted her head and nodded.

"Okay then, I'm going downstairs to get the car ready," Jessica said before leaving the office.

On her exit, Anson entered and went to Deidra.

"Is everything okay?" he asked.

"Yeah. Just they moved the match up an hour and I…"

Anson placed his hand on her shoulder. "We're going to get them, don't worry."

"I know."

"Come here," Anson said before pulling Deidra toward him for a quick embrace. "Just follow the plan," he said as he nudged her to arm's length.

Deidra nodded.

"I'm here if you need anything," he said on his way out the door.

As Deidra turned to me, I looked at the papers as if I didn't hear or see anything that took place.

She approached me. "So, do you have it now?"

I gave her the dossier. "All of it."

"Here," she said, reaching into her pocket and producing a driver's license.

I took it. It was a Texas license with my picture, cover name and the usual information on it.

Deidra sighed. "Okay, Orlando Black, let's get you downstairs. Your ride is in the parking garage."

"Who?" I said.

Deidra stared at me as wrinkles crossed her forehead. "Oh, very good," she said with a slight chuckle. "I was just testing you. Let's go, Mr. Anthony White."

When Deidra and I made it to the parking garage, I went to my car and opened the passenger's side door. I took some cash out of my wallet and stuffed the bills into my pocket before placing the wallet into my glove compartment. I locked the car, then walked to Deidra.

"I don't want to see a single scratch on my car," I said, handing her my keys.

She tilted her head. "Don't worry, it'll be safe here. I won't let anything happen to your precious car."

I stared at her.

"I promise nothing will happen to your car," she said again. "Do you have anything else on you?"

I knelt and lifted my right pants' hem, exposing one of my dual knife holsters strapped around my ankle. "Just these. But they stay with me."

Deidra shook her head. "I don't know, Black."

"I'll take them off before my fight. Plus, it won't hurt to have a little extra protection while undercover. Having knives won't raise a lot of suspicion for a guy like Anthony White, but him not having any weapons at all, just might."

"Fine, you can keep them. I doubt it'll hurt your cover—just be careful."

"Always."

Deidra parted her lips to speak, but before she could, the rev of an engine flowed from behind me. I turned to find Jessica sitting at the wheel of a dented, silver Ford Focus. She winked at me before parking and exiting the car.

"Your ride's here," she said.

I smiled. "Will it make it?"

Jessica shrugged. "Vargas has a… modest cover."

I shook my head and circled to the front of the car. The

hood needed a fresh coat of paint. The headlights were fogged, and the windshield cracked.

As I continued inspecting, Deidra and Jessica chitchatted. I paid little attention to what was being said because the bald tires on the Focus had my attention. I kept my eyes on the front passenger's side tire until I heard Vargas' voice. He wore blue jeans and a wrinkled black shirt as he approached Deidra and Jessica.

"Are we ready?" he asked.

Deidra looked at me. "Are you ready, Black?"

I shrugged. "You haven't given me much of a choice, so yeah, I guess I am."

She exhaled, and the energy drained from her face as she stared at me.

"Well, let's go," Vargas said, opening the driver's side door.

I did the same on the passenger's side before looking back at Deidra. "Was there something else you wanted to tell me?"

She shook her head.

I hunched my shoulders and joined Vargas inside the car, where the scent of vanilla fused with exhaust struck my nose.

"You boys be careful," Jessica said as Vargas put the car in gear and cruised out of the parking garage.

Two minutes later, we were on the highway.

Vargas looked at me. "Black, I'm glad you're on the team."

I winced. "Team? You realize my hand was forced, right?"

"It's nothing personal. It's just this case means a lot to Deidra."

"I can see that—I want to know why."

Vargas shrugged. "It's complicated, not sure I completely understand myself."

I shook my head before turning to my window to watch the power lines and houses roll by.

"What about you?" I asked, still looking out of my window. "Why is this case so important to you?"

"It's my job," Vargas said with a chuckle. "These people are involved in some bad stuff, and I want to stop them. Plus, after working undercover for nearly two months, I'm feeling really vested."

I looked at Vargas as he stared through the windshield. He seemed honest. I believed what he told me but knew there was something even deeper motivating him to close this case.

"How often do you see your family?" I asked.

He glanced at me before looking back at the road. "Not often enough," he said with a sigh. "But anyhow. From this moment forward, you're no longer Orlando Black."

"Got it. I'm Anthony White."

"Exactly. And I'm Hector Corrales," Vargas said before coughing, then buzzing his window down.

"You okay?" I asked.

"Yeah, just this exhaust smell can get strong on the driver's side." Vargas pointed at a small, yellow paper tree hanging from the interior rear-view mirror. "I put this car freshener in to help, and it does, but sometimes the smell is overpowering."

I buzzed down my window.

"But yeah, I'm Hector Corrales, and I met you at a bar last night. A fight broke out and you handled yourself well, so I thought you'd be the perfect contender."

"That's it?"

"Yeah, pretty much. We don't know a lot about each other. I'll let them look into your background themselves. The tech guys at the agency are great with setting up covers, so you'll be fine as long as you know your cover story front and back. You memorized it, right?"

"I did."

"Good. And you have the driver's license for your cover?"

"I do."

"We should be all set, then."

"What's the name of the bar?"

Vargas squinted at me. "What?"

"The bar where we met. What's the name of it?"

"Oh, it's called the Snake Pit. And there was an actual bar fight there last night."

"Do you know the owner?"

"Some guy who goes by the name Big Dale."

"Was he there last night?"

"Yes, our sources confirm he was. Good questions. You really wanna sell this, huh?"

"I really wanna stay alive."

"Don't worry about that. We got you covered."

I looked at him. "Do you?"

Vargas glanced at me. "Of course we do. I know Deidra can be tough, but she wouldn't really—" he said before briefly locking eyes with me. "She won't let anything happen to you," he finished, while facing the windshield.

"I'm not worried about anything happening to me."

"Seems like it."

I shook my head. "Just being careful. Being careful keeps you alive. Worrying doesn't. And if at any point I feel you guys aren't being careful with this operation, I'll leave and you'll never see me again."

Vargas stared at me.

I stared back. "Yeah, those little charges Deidra threatened me with…not worried about 'em."

"Then why would you go through with this?"

"I don't like things lingering over me. You know, unfinished business. And I'm partly responsible for *obstructing* your investigation. Don't like to leave things a mess. Plus, something about this case has really piqued my interest."

"Piqued your interest? This is not a field trip. These are dangerous people, Black."

"I know that. But they're still just people. Which means they have strengths, weaknesses, things they love, and things they hate. We have to be careful and patient enough to learn what they are; if we want the mission to be a success."

"As simple as that, huh? Easy peasy."

"No, people at their core are simple, but this won't be easy."

We drove for another couple of miles before turning onto a poorly paved side road. The Focus hummed up the road for another mile where Vargas made a right turn onto a dirt road. In the distance, I saw a few hangars surrounded by a fence.

"Is this an airport?" I asked.

Vargas nodded at the wheel. "It's an old, abandoned airport, and one venue for these low-level fights."

As we made it closer to the old airport, Vargas slowed. The chain-linked fence rolled by on our right with signs that warned us we were on private property and shouldn't trespass. Twenty-five yards ahead I saw a gated entrance. Standing on either side of the entrance were two muscular men.

Vargas looked at me. "Don't forget, I'm Hector Corrales and you're Anthony White. Remember your cover and how we met," he said, concern in his voice. "And let me do all the talking."

I shrugged.

Vargas made a right turn, then stopped the car before pushing the gearshift into park.

The two men approached. One on Vargas' side and the other on mine. The man approaching Vargas had messy hair and was shorter than his partner. I watched as the guy on my side stared at me through the window before he scratched his buzzed hair and inspected the inside of the car.

Vargas rolled down his window. "Hi Juan, what's up?"

Juan fixed on Vargas' face and squinted. As he stepped closer to the car, he smiled. "Que pasa, Hector. Haven't seen you in a minute."

"Yeah, been busy, tryna' hustle."

"I hear ya—I hear ya."

The guy on my side, the one with the buzz cut, walked past my window. As he did, I saw the butt of a gun tucked in his front waistband. It was a Smith & Wesson 5906. Weight, about thirty-eight ounces. Magazine capacity, fifteen rounds. Well made and rarely jammed. All in all, a great firearm. But considering its jagged design, it may not be the best handgun to have tucked in your pants.

"So, you here to fight?" Juan asked Vargas.

"No, no, I'm not competing."

"You know what? I heard you got whupped by those soft white boys—the ones that the higher-ups sent to recruit."

"I was—there was two of 'em…"

Juan laughed. "It's okay, man," he said, while arching down and patting Vargas on the shoulder. "You know them boys ain't gonna let you sit at their table. Stick with these smaller fights. We gotcha." He looked at me. "Who's this?"

Vargas glanced at me and said, "He's a fighter."

Juan looked me up and down. "Okay, what's your name, Mr. Fighter?"

"White, Anthony White," I said.

"You look like you're in shape, but that doesn't mean much. Are you any good?"

"Is he," Vargas cut in. "I saw him beat two guys like it was nothing."

"Really? Is that true? You can beat two men at once?"

I shrugged. "Maybe even more."

Juan laughed, then stood from the car as the man with the buzz cut approached him.

"It looks clean. Just need to check the trunk," he told Juan before looking at Vargas. "Pop the trunk."

Vargas reached for the trunk's latch.

Juan gestured for him to stop. "Nah, don't worry about it. Hector's good, man. Ya'll go'on through," he said.

"See ya around, Juan," Vargas said.

"Fo'sho. And Mr. Fighter," Juan said, bending down and looking at me. "Good luck."

I shrugged and faced the windshield.

Juan laughed and stood from the car. "Go'on through," he said, patting the hood of the Focus.

Vargas dragged the gear stick to drive, and we pulled off. Clouds of dust encompassed the car as we drove across the dirt. The car rocked along the path for two minutes until we reached the tarmac. We passed two small hangars on our way to a larger one near the back. The large sliding doors were open and nearly twenty cars sat parked around the hangar.

"Quite the turnout for a small fight," I said.

"Sometimes it's even more people than this," Vargas said.

We parked just off the tarmac, somewhat away from the other cars. Vargas exited the car first. When I exited, I circled to his side and we walked toward the front sliding doors. Chanting and hip-hop music flowed from inside. At the front stood a tall, bulky man with his arms folded and a mean look on his face. He nodded at Vargas as if he knew him, then gestured for us to enter the hangar. The smell of nicotine stuffed the air, and a crowd surrounded a mat at the center of the hangar. Everyone in the mob was shouting, clapping, or fist pumping.

"Looks like the first match has already started," Vargas said.

We threaded through the crowd until we found a spot where we could observe the fight. On the mat, two men dressed in jeans and t-shirts threw wild punches and kicks at each other. I shook my head at how sloppy and unintentional their attacks were. Even the referee shook his head while keeping his distance as the two men duked it out.

Vargas looked at me. "What?" he asked, wide eyed. "Are you concerned?"

I scoffed. "No."

"Okay. Just making sure. This type of fighting is very barbaric and can intimidate even the best of fighters."

"I'll be fine. Trust me."

"Let's get you checked in."

We weaved through the horde of people and to the back of the hangar, where there was a booth. Behind the window stood a stocky man with missing teeth.

"Hector, long time no see," the man said as we approached.

"Yeah, I've been busy," Vargas said.

"Busy doing what? Tryna' enter the high-ticket circuit?"

Vargas hunched his shoulders but said nothing.

The man behind the window chuckled. "It's okay. We won't hold it against you. I heard your try-outs didn't go too well though."

"News sure travels fast."

"That's the business. So, are you here to fight?"

Vargas shook his head. "Oh no, I'm not," he said before looking at me. "But I do have a fighter."

The stocky man craned toward the window and looked me up and down. His nose crinkled, and he shrugged. "I've seen plenty of fighters come through here and this one's hard to read. Is he any good?"

"He's better than good," Vargas said.

"Okay. What's your name, fighter?" the man asked me.

"White, Anthony White," I said.

The man's lips protruded, and he kissed the few teeth he had. "Okay, White. You're up next. You'll have fifteen minutes to get ready. Lockers and warm-up equipment is in the back," he said before looking at Vargas. "How much are you putting on your fighter, Hector?"

"Three stacks," Vargas said.

The stocky man's eyes widened. "Three grand? Are you sure? That's a lot to put up for a walk-in. Especially when he's fighting against Butch."

Vargas' eyebrows knitted. "Wait-wait-wait, Butch is here? He's one of the best fighters in this circuit."

The heavy-set guy nodded. "I know," he said while looking down and writing.

"Okay, well, maybe we should hold off until a later match."

"Sorry Hector, you know the rules. I've already filled out the paperwork and this is the only match I can get him in." The man slid a piece of paper under the window.

Vargas looked at me and sighed before reaching into his pocket, removing a wad of bills, and sliding them under the window.

"Thank you," the man said with a grin. "You got about fifteen minutes to get ready while the current fight finishes, and I get the bets in for your match."

"Yeah, we heard you the first time," Vargas said to the man before turning to me. "This way."

We walked toward a hall, and as we did, Vargas hung his head and his eyes wandered.

"Something you want to share with me?" I asked.

Vargas lifted his head and looked around before stepping closer to me. "Butch is a good fighter, Black."

"Yeah, so?"

"I-I think you can beat him, but if you get hurt, you'll need time to recover—"

"And I wouldn't be ready for the big fight in three days," I said.

"Exactly."

"I guess I better not get hurt then."

Vargas took in a breath, then exhaled slowly. "The restroom and equipment is this way," he said while walking down the hall.

I followed him to the end of the hall where we made a left past a concrete partition and into a room. Inside were lockers, sinks, benches, showers, weights, and punching bags.

"What do you need to get ready?" Vargas asked me.

I shrugged. "Not much. Do they have any toilets here?"

"Yeah, at the back, make a right," Vargas said while pointing.

I walked to the back of the room and made a right into a section with four urinals and two toilet stalls. I used the urinal, then walked back to the locker area and washed my hands. Vargas was still standing there.

"So, are you good?" he asked me.

"I'm fine. Why don't you sit down and relax?" I said.

Vargas took a seat on a bench.

I removed the flip phone and my ankle knife holsters and gave them to him. "Hold on to these."

Vargas eyed the knives. "Where did these come from?"

"Just make sure I get them back after the fight."

"Sure, whatever."

I rotated my hips, then tilted my neck from side-to-side before arching and touching my toes. I saw Vargas staring at me as I performed lunges.

"Is there an issue?" I asked.

Vargas shook his head and looked away.

"Just relax," I said to him before throwing a few jabs and kicks at the punching bag.

I concluded my warm-ups by raising my arms above my head on a long inhale, then circling them down with a slow exhale. I did this ten times.

"Okay, I'm ready," I said to Vargas.

He winced at me. "That's it?"

"That's it. Just wanted to loosen my body a little."

"Are you sure?"

"Positive. Now let's go."

We left the locker room and walked through the crowd toward the mat. The referee stood at the center, watching as we approached. When we reached the corner of the mat, Vargas tapped my shoulder.

"Wait here until the ref calls you on the mat," he said.

I nodded.

I looked to the opposite corner and saw a guy with a wide head and muscular frame sporting a red wife-beater and dark-blue jeans. The man threw a few jabs at the air.

"That's Butch," Vargas said. "Like I told you, he's a good fighter. I'm sure most everyone put their money on him. So, what do you think? You think you can beat him?"

I watched as Butch continued to throw jabs and noticed he always dropped his left arm after throwing a jab with it. "Don't worry. I got it," I said to Vargas.

"Okay."

A woman stepped onto the mat and handed the referee a microphone. She caught a lot of the men's eyes on her way and held them as she stood next to the referee.

The ref put the microphone to his lips, and the speakers scratched as he looked and pointed in my direction. "In the black corner we have a new challenger," he started. "He has no fight history and goes by the name White."

Over half the crowd booed.

"Yeah, I don't like that name either," the referee said. "I think we'll call him… um… Ghost!"

"That sounds about right," a man from the crowd shouted. "Because that's what Butch's gonna make him." The man laughed.

I glanced at Vargas. "Friendly crowd," I said under my breath.

The referee then pointed to Butch. "In the red corner, we have one of the top contenders in this circuit. The man slaying, wild animal taming, Butch!"

Butch threw his hands in the air, and most of the crowd cheered.

"Fighters, step on the mat."

Both Butch and I walked to the center. The woman stepped back as we approached the referee. He dropped the microphone to his side and looked at both of us as we stared at each other.

"Make this a good fight. No dirty low-blows, no eye-gouging, no biting. Remember to protect yourself at all times. Break."

I walked back to my corner, and Butch did the same. Once there, Butch slid into a fighting stance and raised his fists. I didn't bother to. The referee then pointed at Butch, and he nodded. He did the same to me, and I nodded.

"Let's fight!" he shouted into the microphone before handing it to the woman, who quickly exited the mat.

I walked about five feet from my corner before Butch raced toward me. I stepped back a foot to keep him at jabbing distance, then waited. Butch threw a right punch, and I parried it. He then followed up with the attack I was waiting for. A left jab. I bobbed under the punch and ended up on his left side, and just as I expected, he dropped his arm. I delivered a hard hook to his left jaw, and he collapsed to the mat. The cheers and yells from the crowd died, and the hangar went completely silent as I turned and walked off the mat.

Vargas' mouth hung open with the whites of his eyes exposed.

I patted him on the shoulder. "Hey, let's go."

He broke out of his trance, and we threaded through the mob with wide eyes staring at us. The speakers scratched and the referee's voice came through.

"Ah… and the winner of this fight by knockout, Ghost!"

The hangar remained silent as Vargas and I walked toward the back booth. As we approached, the stocky man with the missing teeth shook his head.

"I… I don't believe it," he said. "The fight is already over?"

Vargas grinned. "Yep, and I believe you owe me some money. What were the odds?"

The man sighed. "Most bets were on Butch, but we can only do a max of twenty-five to one."

"So three thousand times twenty-five. That's seventy-five thousand."

The man grunted. "I can count, Hector," he said before squatting behind the booth and fiddling with what sounded like keys.

A few moments later, the man stood with a bag and eight stacks of bills.

"Ten, twenty, thirty, forty, fifty, sixty, seventy, five," the stocky man counted as he placed the stacks inside the bag.

He then dropped the bag in a compartment to his right and pushed a lever. A chute door opened on our side, and Vargas grabbed the bag.

"Nice doing business with you," he said to the man.

"Yeah, whatever," the man said. "Hey fighter, who are you?" he asked me as Vargas and I turned to leave.

I looked over my shoulder. "I already told you. Anthony White."

"Yeah, but who are you?"

"Let's just stick with what the ref called me: Ghost," I said before following Vargas out of the hangar.

CHAPTER
FIVE

"YOU SHOULD'VE SEEN him, Deidra," Vargas said into his wireless ear piece as he veered the Focus onto the highway. "He knocked out a top contender with one punch."

I glanced at him and shook my head as I finished strapping my knife holster around my ankle.

"Never seen anything like it," Vargas continued. He listened for a few moments. "No, no, I haven't heard from anyone yet, but everyone there was speechless." Vargas paused again and listened. "Yeah, we're on our way to the motel now. ... Sure, I'll let you know when I'm headed back. ... Of course, I'll be bringing the earnings back with me. ... Alright, talk to you then, bye." He ended the call and looked at me with an enormous grin. "Things are off to a great start."

I said nothing.

"Don't you think?" Vargas asked.

"Maybe. You said Butch was one of the best fighters in this circuit. Do you know if he's ever fought in the high-ticket matches?"

Vargas shook his head. "I don't believe he has," he said with his eyes on the road.

"So, they don't believe he's good enough for it?"

"Getting into those matches is political. It's about money. Although he's not on your level, Butch is a great fighter for this circuit, but he still has that thug-like demeanor."

"So, they're looking for someone who fights well, but with a certain elegance."

"Exactly."

"Seems it'll be hard for them to find someone like that in this circuit. The fighters I've seen so far are rough around the edges, unpolished."

"Well, that's certainly not you. I'm sure word about your performance today will get back to them fast."

"That's what I'm afraid of," I said under my breath.

"What's that?"

"Nothing."

Vargas glanced at me before shrugging, then placing his attention back on the road. We drove for another fifteen minutes before he turned off the main road and onto the motel's driveway. The motel was a two-story structure made of orange brick. The stairs and railing were white with chipped paint, and the parking lot was virtually empty. Including the Focus, there were only four cars in the entire lot. Vargas wheeled the car into a spot.

"Here's your new home. For the next few days at least," he said.

I said nothing, and continued to survey the area.

"I know it's not the Ritz-Carlton," Vargas continued. "But you'll be on the first level. Room 6A," he finished before handing me a key. "Remember Black, you're now Anthony White and I'm Hector Corrales."

"I got it."

"Just making sure. My number's programmed in the flip phone Jessica gave you earlier. It's under Hector, so when we're on the phone, we only talk about things that Anthony and Hector would talk about. Nothing concerning the operation. If you need to provide operation specific details—"

"Wait to talk with you in person or call Deidra's number that I memorized because the line will be encrypted," I interrupted.

"Right, and—"

"If things get really sticky or I can't reach you, leave a message in the mailbox at either of the locations that I also memorized. Got it."

Vargas sighed. "I just want to make sure we cover all of our bases."

"Understood."

Vargas dug into his pocket and produced a small wad of cash. "Here's some spending money, for food and what not."

I took the wad and stuffed it into my pocket. "Is that it? Are all the bases covered now?" I said.

Vargas nodded.

"Alright. I'll see you around," I said as I opened my door.

"You know what?" Vargas said. "I'll walk in with you, just to check out the room."

I shrugged. "Okay," I said before exiting the car and shutting the door.

The room was at the far west corner of the building. I inserted the key in the door and rotated it until I heard a click, then turned the knob and pushed the door open. Inside was a queen-size bed, a dresser with a television resting on top, a desk, and a microwave. Whoever made the bed made it without a single wrinkle in the comforter, and the faint scent of cleaning solution lingered in the air.

"Better than what I was expecting," I said.

"Yeah, they've been slowly renovating this building," Vargas said as he closed the door.

I looked down and noticed vinyl flooring running from the living area into the bathroom. "Definitely better than some motels I've seen."

Vargas walked to the bathroom briefly, and when he returned, he opened the dresser drawers and peeked inside each. One by one. "There's some change of clothes in the drawers. Mainly jeans and t-shirts. Should fit you. Oh, and there's some workout clothes just in case, you know, you wanna workout."

"Thanks."

Vargas scanned the room once more before walking to the door. "Alright, I'm out. I'll be in touch when I have your next fight. Be careful, Black."

I winced. "Black, who's that?"

Vargas chuckled on his way out. I closed, then locked the door behind him. The first thing I wanted to do was get a lay of the land, but before I did, I figured I'd make sure my current channel of communication was operational. I removed the phone from my pocket and flipped it open. The battery showed fully charged, and I was getting three bars of signal. *We're good there*, I thought as I opened the top dresser drawer. A new pack of boxer briefs, socks, and t-shirts lay inside. In the drawer below were jeans, and in the last drawer was some activewear, like Vargas said. The bathroom had all the linen I needed, and a box of toothpaste and a new tooth-brush, sat on the counter next to the sink. *I guess the DEA is doing something right.*

I stepped out of the room, ensured the door locked shut, then walked to the opposite end of the motel. It was quiet, and I only saw one other person around the building. I looked up the road and noticed a sign for a diner about a quarter of a mile away. I walked in that direction, figuring it would be best to eat while I could. After walking the quarter of a mile, I came to an old one-story building with boarded doors and windows. A metal plaque with five numbers etched in it hung above the door. I recognized the number as one of the two addresses I memorized for the secure drop locations. I looked around and noticed a blue, rusted mail drop box with two locks on the back of it, bolted to a concrete foundation.

I shrugged. *Found one of 'em.*

The diner was twenty-five yards up the road on the opposite side of the highway. A small establishment with little parking, which was fine by me considering I didn't have a car. I pulled the door open, and a bell dinged as I entered. Directly in front of me sat a bar top with stools lined in front of it, and on the other side of the bar top, two cooks occupied the kitchen. One was heavy-set, and he looked at me as he wiped his hand across his apron.

"We'll be with you in a minute. Have a seat anywhere you like. Kelly!" he said.

I nodded and looked to my right. Booths ran the length of the restaurant all the way to the restroom at the end. To the left was the same, but instead of a bathroom at the end, there was an isolated booth. *Bingo.* I proceeded across the checkered tiled floor and the scent of burgers, fries, and ketchup hit my nose as I passed a family of four sitting in a booth. I nodded and the father and mother returned the gesture. As I sat at my booth, a door near the kitchen flapped open and a middle-aged woman with silky dirty-blonde hair entered the dining room. She rolled her eyes at the heavy-set cook before pacing over to me with a menu in hand.

"Evening, sir. My name is Kelly and I'll be serving you," she said, handing me the menu. "What can I start you off with to drink?"

I quickly glanced over the menu and considered a burger and fries but thought about it and decided on something a little more appropriate for my current situation. "I'll just have a water, and I know what I want," I said.

Kelly smiled. "Awesome. That was quick. So, what can I get for you?"

"I'll have your grilled chicken, brown rice, and steamed broccoli."

"Oh, the healthy choice."

"Yeah, trying to watch my figure."

Kelly smiled and glanced me over. "Your figure looks fine to me," she said while extending her hand.

I returned the smile and passed her the menu.

She tucked it under her arm. "I'll get that in for you, Mr...."

"White. Anthony White," I said.

Kelly smiled again. "Okay, Mr. White. I'll be back with your water."

I nodded then watched as she walked away and disappeared behind the same door she had entered. A minute later, she returned with a cup of water.

"There you go," she said as she sat it on the table. "Anything else?" she asked while placing a straw next to the cup.

"No, I think I'm good for now," I said.

Kelly returned to the kitchen and talked with the heavyset cook. The two exchanged words before she shook her head, threw a hand in the air, and walked through the door again.

I shrugged, then peeled the paper from my straw before dropping the straw into my cup and taking a sip. Before I could take a second sip, I felt a vibration in my pocket. The words *unknown number* displayed on the flip phone.

"Hello," I answered.

"Hi Black, this is Deidra. What are you doing? Can you talk?"

"Grabbing an early dinner. And yes, I can talk."

"Great. I spoke with Vargas today, and things are off to an excellent start. Great job."

"Thank you, I guess."

"You may not think so, but we're doing good work here."

"No, I believe these people are bad and need to be taken down. It's just the methods. Something's off, and I'll find out what it is. I always do."

The line with silent for a moment.

Deidra sighed. "I'm not sure what you're hoping to find, but I'm just doing my job here."

"I don't doubt that," I said, then immediately thought, *Just not sure of your motivations.*

"Okay then. Do you need anything or—"

"Nope."

"Well, enjoy your dinner and have a good evening. Make sure you get some rest. There's no telling when Vargas could have another fight lined up for you."

"Got it. Talk with you later."

"Bye."

I ended the call, placed the phone in my pocket, then sat with my thoughts for twenty minutes. During that time, the restaurant's population increased by fifty percent.

Kelly came to my table and set my plate down. "It smells good," she said. "I think I might have the same thing at the end of my shift."

"You always work this shift?" I asked.

"Yeah, but only for a few hours, so I'll be getting off soon."

"You like it here?"

Kelly shrugged. "It's okay, I guess. Just working here for a little extra money. During the day I work at the mall." She pointed. "Half a mile up the road. Then walk here to work for a few hours."

I nodded. "Busy day."

"It can be. Anything else I can get for you, Mr. White?" she asked.

"No, I'm okay for now, thanks."

"Okay, let me know if you need anything," she said with a smile before walking away toward a recently occupied booth.

It took me less than twenty minutes to clean my plate. I sat for a minute to let my food digest, then dropped enough cash on the table to cover the meal and leave Kelly a twenty-dollar tip. On my way out of the diner, she waved at me.

"Nice to meet you. Have a good night, bye."

I waved back and exited the diner.

The sun dipped toward the horizon and the sky was dark by the time I made it back to my room. I removed the contents of my pockets and placed them near the clock on the nightstand next to the bed. Figuring I better follow Deidra's advice and get some rest while I could, I took off my shoes, washed my hands and face, brushed my teeth, then plopped on the bed and closed my eyes.

When I opened them next, the clock displayed 4:30 a.m. I sat up and took in a deep breath before standing, stretching, then dropping to the floor and performing one hundred push-ups, followed by the same number of sit-ups. Once finished, I stood from the floor and shadow boxed, then performed some judo and wrestling drills I learned as a teenager. The clock now showed 5:42 a.m., and I wanted to conclude my workout with some form practice, but there wasn't enough room inside, so I threw on a sweatshirt and a pair of sweatpants and stepped outside into the darkness. At the end of the motel was a small, dimly lit field. Perfect for what I needed. I started with a karate form I learned as a kid, then a Shaolin Kung Fu form I learned during my time in China, and concluded with tai chi. After I went back to the room, showered, and dressed, the clock displayed 7:16 a.m., and I was thinking about breakfast.

I went back to the same diner where I ate the night before. Saw the same heavy-set cook in the kitchen. And sat at the same booth. It was practically the same experience except a freckled-faced young man in his early twenties served me. After my meal, I made the half-mile walk to the mall. It was a large, off-white building composed of various restaurants, clothing stores, and shops. I concluded it was the spot where everyone conducted their business because surrounding the mall were grocery stores, more restaurants, banks, and department stores. The cars in the mall's parking lot were sparse. I figured the mall was closed, so I walked across the street to a coffee shop and ordered a green tea despite my craving for a coffee. I sat with my cup and thought maybe I was too nice for jumping in and helping Vargas during his little audition. Sipping the tea, my mind went to the big fight that was now only two days away. I sighed, then seriously considered going back to the DEA HQ, getting into my car, and leaving town, but as I took another sip, I thought about all the innocent people the Cartels had hurt.

Yeah, too nice.

After sitting with my thoughts for another half hour, I left the coffee shop and headed across the street to the mall. The parking lot began to fill, and many people walked toward the building. I entered the mall through a sporting goods store and immediately a leather-rubbery scent hit my nose. As I walked past a rack of canoes and a rack of fishing rods and reels, I heard scraping coming from my right. A short man with gray on his face and head was pulling a pallet of boxes. When he saw me, he stopped, squinted, then walked toward me.

"How you doing, sir? Anything I can help you find?" he asked.

I shook my head. "No. Just looking around."

The man smiled. "Okay," he said, nodding his head. "Are you an outdoorsman?"

I shrugged. "Sometimes."

"What? Do you hunt?"

I nodded. "Yeah, I do a little hunting from time to time."

"Oh great! Now we don't sell guns in the store, but upstairs," the man said while pointing at some stairs, "we have a new selection of crossbows and bows and arrows."

"I may just have to check that out," I said.

"Okay, let me know if you need help with anything," he said on his way back to his pallet.

I continued through the store and out to the mall's main concourse. The sound of footsteps and voices immediately struck my ears. There was a shoe store to my left and a jewelry store to my right, and four yards in front of me, a young woman at a kiosk selling sunglasses to a woman wearing a strapless white and blue summer dress. I walked past and made a left where more stores flanked me on both sides. I counted six people walking ahead of me, two behind me, and a few entering and exiting the stores. It all reminded me why I really didn't enjoy going to malls. There were only a handful of people, but they were coming from multiple directions all at once. I could only imagine what it'd be like with the mall packed; threat detection would become a challenge.

I passed a playground area and into a food court where most of the restaurants were closed or just opening. After circling the food court, I walked back in the direction I came, past the hall for the sporting goods store and to the opposite side of the mall. It was more of the same. More shops, more kiosks, more people, and more headache for me. As I turned to leave, something caught my eye, or rather, someone. Kelly, the waitress from the morning before, stood outside of a shoe store, but she wasn't alone. Standing next to her was someone I'd seen two days prior. One of the men Vargas duked it out with, Ethan Long.

Whatta ya know.

I slipped behind a kiosk and pretended to admire the assortment of candles while watching the two converse from my peripheral. Long said something while Kelly shrugged and shook her head before saying something back with squinted eyes. Long hunched his shoulders, then Kelly shrugged again before pivoting toward the store and waving at him. He waved back before walking in my direction. I faced the shelf of candles and inhaled a vanilla scent while Long's footsteps knocked past me. The blond spiky-haired man continued down the concourse before making a left and disappearing from my sight.

I entered the shoe store and saw Kelly as she walked down the center aisle and to the back. As I strolled down the aisle, perusing the shelves on either side of me, a thin, young man with dark hair and pale skin approached me. He wore a black polo shirt with the store's logo embroidered on it.

"Anything I can help you with?" he asked.

"Naw, just looking," I said.

"Okay, I'll be at the register if you need anything."

I nodded, then walked to the men's section. A moment later, Kelly returned from the back wearing the same shirt as the store clerk. As she walked past me, I turned to a pair of boots, picked one up, and pretended to inspect it. She went to the register and had a word with her co-worker. The two laughed, and then she walked back in my direction. I sat the boot down and stepped into the center aisle as she was coming. Kelly paused as I glanced at her, smiled, then continued to the opposite side of the aisle.

"Excuse me," she said to my back.

I glanced over my shoulder and squinted as if I didn't recognize her.

"Hi," she said.

"Hey, hi, um…"

"I waited on you yesterday—at the diner."

"Right."

"Mr. White. Anthony, right?"

"Yeah, and you're Kelly, um… Long," I said, taking a shot in the dark at the last name.

She squinted and tilted her head. "I told you my last name?"

I shrugged, and she smiled.

"But yeah," she continued. "You always come to the mall this early? The store just opened like ten minutes ago." She smiled.

"I'm somewhat of an early bird."

"I'll say. You nearly beat me here."

"No, I think you got here before me. I saw you standing outside talking with your boyfriend," I said.

Kelly winced. "No, no, no. That was my older brother, Ethan."

You don't say. "Oh, sorry. My mistake."

"No worries. He's been hassling me about walking to work. Even offered to buy me a new car—my current car is in the shop."

"That's nice of him."

Kelly hunched her shoulders. "Yeah, but I like to do things on my own."

"You don't like owing anyone. I get that."

"He said I wouldn't owe him, but I just want to make my own way."

"Your brother must have a great job."

Kelly nodded. "He started a new job about three months ago. Not exactly sure what it is—I think he mentioned he's some kinda recruiter, but anyway."

"Maybe I should become a recruiter," I said.

"No kidding. He seems to make good money, but I think the job may be stressing him out."

"What makes you say that?"

"I don't know," she said with a shrug. "He's just always on edge."

I nodded.

"But anyway, whatta 'bout you?"

"Me? I'm just here looking at shoes."

Kelly smiled. "Anything you like?"

"Those boots over there caught my eye, but I'm not ready to get 'em just yet."

A group of young women entered the store.

"Well, you have customers to tend to," I said.

"Yeah…"

"Are you working at the diner tonight?"

"Yep. I'll be there."

"Okay. I might stop by to trouble you for some more grilled chicken."

Kelly smiled. I smiled back and walked toward the entrance.

"Bye, Anthony."

I paused, turned, and waved bye before exiting the store. *Small world.*

THANK YOU FOR READING

I have a favor to ask. If you have a moment, I would really appreciate it if you could leave a short review on the page where you purchased this book. I'm thankful for you sharing your feedback about this book. It really helps new readers find this series.

Sign up for notifications of new books by Alex Cage and exclusive giveaways

www.AlexCage.com/signup

MORE BOOKS BY ALEX CAGE

Orlando Black Series

Carolina Dance

Bayside Boom

Family Famous (Novella)

Bet on Black

Leroy Silver Series

Contracts & Bullets

Aloha & Bullets

Politics Thieves & Bullets

Get the latest releases and exclusive giveaways, sign up to the Alex Cage Reader List.

www.AlexCage.com/signup

AVAILABLE IN AUDIO

Orlando Black Universe

Queen City Ruby (Short Story)

Survival Intuition (A Rose Lee Flash Fiction Story)

Sunshine Scandal (Short Story)

Once You Go Black (Short Story)

Standalone

Bullet Fist Gunn

ABOUT THE AUTHOR

Alex Cage is a thriller author and passionate wordsmith who loves to blend his fascination with martial arts and travel with high-octane action and explosive adventures. He enjoys nothing more than entertaining his readers with death-defying missions, larger-than-life characters, and suspenseful stories that always find a way to keep you on your toes.

As the author of nearly a dozen titles, including the Orlando Black series and the Leroy Silver series, Alex combines his obsession for thrillers with a sprinkling of fantasy and sci-fi, so that readers will always find something to capture their imagination. He currently resides in North Carolina. When not writing his next novel, you can find him reading and practicing martial arts.

Find out more about Alex Cage (and get a free read):

www.alexcage.com
connect@alexcage.com